THE KINGDOMS OF EVERNOW

PREQUEL

HEIDI CATHERINE

SEQUEL HOUSE

For Sonia
A real angel now

The Kingdoms of Evernow

Palace

Wintergreen

Apothecary

The Round

The Sands of Naar

Tavern

The Bay of Laurel

Palace

Mines

Feldspar

Palace

The Arena

Forte Cadence

Aria Flats

Mount Allegro

The Valley of the Blessed

Lighthouse

GABRIELLE

THE BEFORE

*G*abrielle stood outside her tent in the market, letting the wind pick up the fine fabric of her skirt and send it billowing around her legs. Seventeen and all alone in the world. This wasn't what she wanted for herself, but it was what she'd always known would come to be.

A horse and cart rattled past, kicking up dust and Gabrielle shielded her face.

"Fortunes! Get your fortune read!" she called to nobody in particular. There was no need to shout too loudly. If someone's fortune was meant to be read, they'd find her easily enough.

It felt wrong to take money for sharing a gift she firmly felt had been given to her so she could do good in the world. But even angels had to eat. Well, human ones, anyway. And food in the Valley of the Blessed was becoming harder to come by. The people around her were looking more frail, and the fortunes she read were becoming more bleak.

Except for King Virtus. He was looking very robust the last time she'd seen him riding past in his golden carriage with his sad wife and podgy son—a boy also named Virtus— who'd one day become the King of Forte Cadence.

Gabrielle didn't need to read that boy's fortune to know what was in his heart. She could feel the darkness from a hundred paces away, which filled her with worry for the people of her kingdom. Hard times were going to fall. There would be a lot of suffering before the bad could be turned to good, but she believed with all her heart there was happiness in the world out there.

"Fortunes! Get your fortune read!"

A woman she recognized as an old friend of her mother's scurried past, scowling. Gabrielle smiled in return, trying to use joy to chase away the woman's judgment, but it didn't work. It never did. She was used to that. People were either fascinated with her gift or feared it. It was near impossible to sway someone from one side to the other.

She wondered what this woman's judgment would be if she knew Gabrielle's gift had been shared by her mother. A gift she'd kept quiet about, rather than shouting out loud in a busy marketplace. But her mother hadn't been starving. She'd had a husband and a small house and a garden. All things that Gabrielle wanted for herself one day. If she believed the fortune she'd read for herself, she'd have all these things and more. The only problem was that the 'more' included heartbreak, pain and suffering beyond anything she knew how to deal with. Long ago, she'd decided it was far easier to read the fortunes of others and leave her own in the hands of fate.

Gabrielle slipped inside her tent and sat down at the small table she'd set up with a large, round rock covered by a red cloth. She hoped it looked like a crystal ball and so far, nobody had questioned it. The only thing she needed when reading fortunes was herself but had quickly learned that the people who visited her were more comfortable with the strangeness of her gift if they thought it came from a crystal, instead of deep inside an unexplained part of her.

With memories of her mother swirling in her mind's eye, Gabrielle placed her hands on the cold surface of the rock. Her mother had passed her gift onto Gabrielle when she'd died. That was when her visions had bloomed beyond the pale images that used to cross her mind when she slept. She wasn't sure whether to thank her mother or curse her. When the future was filled with hardship, it wasn't necessarily a blessing to be able to see it.

A woman poked her head inside the tent, darting in quickly and checking behind her, before drawing the heavy fabric closed. Most of Gabrielle's customers entered in this same way.

Lifting a scarf to cover her babyish blonde curls, she returned her hands to the rock and allowed her eyelashes to flutter, taking the theatre of the job almost as seriously as the genuine work itself.

"I need you to read my future." The lines on the woman's face deepened with her desperation as she slid onto the seat on the other side of the table.

"Three copper coins and the future is yours." Gabrielle barely lifted her gaze, sensing this woman wouldn't be comfortable with eye contact yet. It would be disappointing if she changed her mind and decided to run.

"This is all I have." The woman placed half a loaf of bread on the table, something that Gabrielle could purchase for one coin alone.

She looked at the bread. It smelled good, and her mouth instantly watered. It wasn't like she had a queue of customers lining up outside her tent. But did this devalue her work? Would this woman return another day with only a quarter loaf? Would she tell others that Gabrielle had lowered her price?

"It is three copper coins," Gabrielle repeated.

"Please," said the woman, pushing the loaf forward. "There are things I need to know."

Gabrielle searched the woman's face, the visions already pouring into her mind as if her empty stomach had given them permission to arrive. There *were* things this woman needed to know.

"Just this one time." Gabrielle moved the bread to the side of the table. "But please don't tell anybody."

"Thank you." The woman's eyes filled with tears.

"Give me your hands." Gabrielle reached out and the woman slipped her palms into her grasp, the worthless rock sitting in the middle of the circle they made. Gabrielle braced herself for the visions to sort themselves out in her mind as the angels decided which one needed to be seen first.

"You have a son," she said.

The woman nodded, her face pursed in conflict, as if she wanted Gabrielle to be the real deal but at the same time, the idea of it disturbed her.

"He's young with dark hair." Gabrielle provided only the details that were necessary to prove what she had to say was true. The color of this woman's son's hair wasn't what was important here.

The woman nodded again, the pupils of her eyes widening slightly.

"He's sick," said Gabrielle, seeing an image of the boy emptying the contents of his stomach into a bucket.

"We don't know what's causing it." The woman shook her head, biting down on her bottom lip as she hung on Gabrielle's words.

"I see a goat," said Gabrielle, not always understanding how some of the things she saw fitted together. "Does that mean anything to you?"

The woman nodded enthusiastically. "We have a goat that provides enough milk for us to all stay healthy. That goat has been keeping my son alive. Without it, we'd have lost him by now. Do you think I should give him more milk?"

Gabrielle shook her head, certain she now knew how the goat fitted with the boy's illness. "That goat will kill your son if he continues to drink her milk. She's not keeping him alive. She's the cause of what's making him ill."

The woman sat back on the small stool she was perched on as her face turned pale. "My entire family drinks that goat's milk! And we're not sick. You're mistaken."

"I'm not mistaken," said Gabrielle firmly. "Your son's body can't process your goat's milk. Give him water for a week and you'll see an immediate improvement."

"You're a fake!" screeched the woman, standing up. "A fake! How dare you tell me I've been poisoning my own son. I'm a good mother! I would never give him anything that would hurt him, let alone kill him."

4

"You didn't do it on purpose," said Gabrielle, gently. "You weren't to know. And you came seeking answers, which makes you a very good mother."

"I made a mistake coming here," the woman sneered.

They glanced at the bread on the table at the same time and Gabrielle slowly reached out her hand toward it. She'd earned that bread! What she'd told this woman was the truth. It wasn't her fault if the woman chose not to believe her.

Before she could get her hand near the loaf, the woman snatched it back and clutched it to her chest.

"Fake!" She spat out the word. "You've seen me with my boy at the market. That's how you knew about him!"

"It's your choice to take back my payment," said Gabrielle, trying her best to keep calm. "But please, stop giving your boy the milk."

As much as she needed the bread, she wasn't going to perish if she went one more day without food. But the boy was different. He didn't have long if his mother continued to force him to drink the one thing that was making him sick.

"You should be ashamed of yourself." The woman lifted the hem of her dress from the grubby dirt floor of the tent and swept out, back into the busy marketplace.

Gabrielle's stomach groaned in protest.

"Don't worry," she said, looking down at her middle. "She'll be back. And next time she'll have far more to offer than half a loaf of bread. We'll eat soon."

"You know that talking to yourself is a sign you're going mad," came a deep voice from the entrance of her tent.

Gabrielle's head snapped up to see a young man. He was around her age. Perhaps a year or two older. Tall and lean with blond hair and eyes the color of midnight, an unusual contrast of shades.

"Aren't all fortune tellers supposed to be mad?" she asked, rolling her eyes. "And the people who visit them."

"Not sure." He grinned. "Your last customer certainly seemed mad, but in a different kind of way."

"Have we met?" she asked, feeling like she'd seen him somewhere before. Although, when you saw the future, sometimes it was hard to tell if a person had been in your past or if they were destined to join you on the road ahead.

"Only in your dreams." He winked at her and took a step inside her tent.

"Do you need your fortune read?" She gave him a tight-lipped smile. "It's three copper coins. No exceptions."

"How about two copper coins and a kiss?" he asked.

She laughed, despite herself. She'd had many inappropriate comments before from customers, but there was something about this guy that was different. Perhaps it was because they were of similar age. Or because of how undeniably handsome he was. Or maybe it was because she suspected his joke was merely intended to set her at ease.

"A kiss would raise the price, not lower it." She crossed her arms and smirked.

"Oh, but you've never had one of my kisses." He attempted to lean on the opening of the tent, stumbling when it bowed and failed to hold his weight. Steadying himself and smoothing out his clothes, he grinned at her.

"Three coins," she said, suppressing a smile. "No kiss."

"Fine. I'd say it's your loss, but we both know it's mine." He took a seat on the stool opposite the table and placed three coins in front of her.

Surprised he'd paid what she'd asked, Gabrielle quickly swooped up the coins and slid them into her pocket.

"Are you sure I can't give you four coins if you throw in a kiss?" he asked.

"I'm sure." She wondered if he was the sort who paid for kisses and everything else that went with those kinds of payments, but somehow, she didn't think so. A good-looking man like him probably had fifty girlfriends. At any rate, she was about to find out, whether she wanted to kiss him or not.

"You're not from the Valley of the Blessed," she said, delaying getting started with his reading but unsure why.

He shook his head. "I'm from Aria Flats. But shouldn't you already know that?"

She raised her eyebrows both at his boldness and his place of birth. Aria Flats was the wealthiest settlement in Forte Cadence. Being from the other side of the kingdom meant she most likely hadn't met this intriguing man before. Then why did she feel like she had?

"I'd definitely remember you if we'd met before," he said. And here she was thinking she was the one doing this reading. Perhaps they should swap seats.

"Give me your hands please," she said, deciding to get on with it.

He remained frozen in his seat. Were there some nerves underneath his bravado?

"Your hands?" she prompted again, curious if there a deeper reason that had brought him to her tent.

He took a deep breath and slipped his hands into hers. She jolted at the sharpness of the vision that fired into her mind. The room spun, then held completely still, and she found herself holding onto him tightly.

Now she knew why he'd delayed this reading.

It was because this vision wasn't good. It made her previous reading with the woman with the goat feel like a warm-up.

She coughed, trying to disguise her shock.

When the future was filled with hardship, it really wasn't a blessing to be able to see it.

CASSIUS

THE BEFORE

*C*assius looked at the beautiful girl across the table, studying her reaction to the contact of their hands.

He'd been to fortune tellers from one end of the kingdom to the other, seeking just one who wasn't a fake. Some would take his hands and smile at him, and he'd know immediately he was wasting his time. Others would look deeply into his eyes and tell him of the great fortune coming his way, and he'd be forced to get up and leave, knowing this couldn't be true.

But not this girl.

She'd sat up straight the moment their hands touched and stared at him, all the mirth of their banter chased away by the sadness that spilled into her eyes.

Those big blue eyes of hers had seen him.

She knew what lay ahead.

Which meant she was anything but a fake.

"What's your name?" he asked.

She hesitated, then seemed to decide the question was innocent enough. "Gabrielle."

It was a suitable name for an angel. And with her soft blonde curls, she definitely looked the part.

"Gabrielle," he repeated, enjoying turning her name over in his mouth. "I'm Cassius."

She let go of his hands as a flush spread across her cheeks, placing them on what was certainly a river rock lying underneath that red cloth.

"You truly see it, don't you?" he asked.

"I see lots of things." Her voice was a whisper now and she focused on the rock, determined to avoid his eye.

"Including my future," he said.

He reached for her hands again, removing them from the rock and holding them as he locked his eyes on her, waiting for her to look up.

"Cassius." She lifted her eyes to his and shook her head, letting go of his hands to reach into her pocket, placing his three coins back on the table. "I'm unable to read your future. I can't see anything. I'm sorry I wasted your time."

He pushed the coins back to her. "Keep them."

She seemed torn as her fingertips hesitated. "But I didn't tell you anything."

"You told me plenty," he said, meaning it. He already had everything he came here for. Proof that he was looking at a genuine angel. There was no mistaking it. And it wasn't because of her delicate features, or the purity of her skin. It was the light behind her eyes. The people who surrounded her in this busy marketplace had no idea who was living amongst them. Gabrielle was the real deal.

"It wouldn't be right." She shook her head, folding her hands in her lap as if to stop herself from accepting his payment.

"Then would you allow me to buy you a meal?" He scooped up the coins and stood.

"I'm not hungry, thank you," she said, seeming to forget he'd heard her speaking to her empty stomach when he'd arrived.

"Please?" He pressed his palms together and held them in front of his chest. "As an apology for wasting my time."

"You want to buy me a meal as an apology for me wasting your time?" She shook her head and he longed to reach out and tuck one of her stray curls behind her ear. "You do realize that makes no sense, don't you?"

"Gabrielle," he said. "After what you just saw, are you denying me my wish to buy you some food?"

"I saw nothing." Her hand fluttered to her cheek, a sure sign of her deception. "I was unable to read you."

"I was thinking soup," he said, holding open the entrance to the tent. "With bread for dipping."

"I told you, I'm not hungry." Gabrielle winced as her stomach grumbled loudly.

Cassius laughed. "Please?"

"Okay." She stood and ran a hand through her hair. "Just one bowl of soup then."

She must be even hungrier than he'd realized.

As she ducked under his outstretched arm to exit the tent, he caught her floral scent and his stomach tightened in a way it never had before. But then again, he'd never met anyone like Gabrielle before.

Not that he could have any future with her. Because she'd seen what he'd somehow always known but had never been able to have confirmed.

Until now.

GABRIELLE

THE BEFORE

*G*abrielle walked beside Cassius as they wove their way through the busy rows of market stalls. They passed half-empty stalls stocked with tired vegetables, and nodded politely at the eager tailors, bakers, blacksmiths and weavers, all desperate to sell them their wares. She hated that she'd gone with Cassius so easily. Accepting this soup meant she was going to owe him. But what was worse—owing a stranger a bowl of soup, or dying of starvation completely debt free?

What she'd seen in her tent had shaken her up. In all the readings she'd done for people, she'd never seen anything like her vision of Cassius's future.

"I hope it's carrot soup," he said, jolting her from her thoughts. "I'm certain I can smell carrots."

Gabrielle sniffed the air, unable to detect anything except dust and depression. "Do carrots even have a smell?"

"No idea, but they help you see." He smiled at her with the kind of grin that had surely broken hearts all over the kingdom. His dark eyes had a way of sparkling that made it impossible not to smile back.

"And what do you see?" she asked him.

"Lots of things." The smile slipped from his eyes. "And I know you saw them, too."

Gabrielle's mouth fell open, but Cassius had planned the timing of his comment well.

"Hot soup!" called an extremely thin woman from behind a giant cooking pot.

"Smells delicious." Cassius placed a hand on the small of Gabrielle's back as he led her to the woman. "What's in it today?"

"Carrot and pumpkin, my love." The woman smiled warmly at him, although Gabrielle suspected it was at the idea of a sale, rather than Cassius's charms.

"Just what I was hoping for," he said.

The woman eyed him suspiciously and Gabrielle knew she was trying to decide on a price based on how much money she thought he had. He'd said he was from Aria Flats, which meant he likely came from a wealthy family. And he had produced those three coins with great ease. But what would a wealthy young man be doing in the Valley of the Blessed?

"I'll take two bowls please," said Cassius.

"Four coins," said the woman. Gabrielle had purchased soup from this woman at less than half that price but admired her for having a try.

"Throw in some of that bread and you have a deal." Cassius winked at her.

The woman smiled once more, revealing a set of rotten teeth. It seemed times were just as tough in the soup business as they were in fortune telling. Perhaps even tougher.

Gabrielle watched as the woman dished the soup into bowls and roughly cut two generous chunks of bread. She sniffed in the delicious aroma, deciding carrots definitely have a smell. As much as she hated that she was now in Cassius's debt, it was going to be good to be able to sleep tonight in the back of her tent without her empty stomach complaining.

Cassius handed the woman four coins and took the soup.

"Don't go running off with my bowls now," the woman warned.

"It's okay," said Gabrielle, pointing to Cassius who was carrying the soup to a table that had been set up off to the side of the woman's stall. "We'll just be here."

"Hot soup!" the woman called, losing interest as she chased her next sale.

"You realize you paid her far too much, don't you?" Gabrielle perched herself on the log that was intended to be used as a stool, trying to balance herself.

"Did I?" Cassius unsuccessfully suppressed a smile.

"She wasn't even nice to us." Gabrielle slurped up her first taste of the soup and savored the flavor, resisting the urge to eat quickly.

"What if she's not nice because she's hungry?" asked Cassius. "It would be torture to serve up soup all day and not be able to eat any of it yourself."

Gabrielle looked at the woman again, seeing her in a somewhat different light. She *did* look hungry. And he was right. That would be torture.

"So, why didn't you buy a third bowl and give it to her?" she asked.

He shrugged. "Maybe she doesn't like carrots. Now she has the coins, she can decide for herself what she'd like to have."

"But what if she spends it on something worthless?" Gabrielle tore off a chunk of bread and dipped it in the soup. "Wouldn't it be better to guarantee food in her belly?"

"Her decision." He grinned at her. "Why do you care so much?"

"I don't really." She shrugged, not wanting to admit how fascinated she was by his view of the world.

He set down his bread and tilted his head at her from across the table.

"What's wrong?" She wiped her mouth with the back of her hand, worried she had soup smudged across her cheek.

"Do you have friends?" He picked his bread back up and bit into it.

She looked down at her soup and swirled her spoon. Cassius had hit a nerve. She didn't have friends. She had people she was friendly with, but that's where it ended. It's hard to find people to trust when you live in a sea of such hopelessness. Besides, people didn't want to be friends with someone like Gabrielle. She was different to everyone else. This made her mother's death even harder to deal with. She often wondered if she was the only angel left on Earth.

"I have friends," she lied, still avoiding his gaze. "Besides, I don't exactly see you traveling around here with a group of companions."

Now it was his turn to wince, and he concentrated on his soup with such gusto that she almost felt guilty.

"Who are you?" she asked. "What are you doing here?"

He put down his spoon and focused his full attention on her. "I was looking for you. Except I didn't know it was you. Well, not until… you knew it was me."

This shouldn't have made sense, and she hated that it did.

Because the vision she'd seen was of Cassius's death. And while it had saddened her, that hadn't been what had bothered her so much. She'd seen death plenty of times in her readings—more and more often lately in the Valley of the Blessed—and usually she dealt with it by providing the kind of advice she believed would help the person live their remaining days in peace. Or perhaps encourage them to take a different path to stave off death, like the woman with the sick son.

But the vision of Cassius had been different. She hadn't just seen his death. She'd seen herself beside his bed, holding his cold hand as she'd wept the kind of agonizing tears that are only shed when your heart is broken. And she hadn't looked any older.

Which meant he didn't have much time left.

They ate the rest of their soup in silence. Sometimes when there are too many words to say, it's best not to speak any of them out loud.

CASSIUS

THE BEFORE

*C*assius knew he had no right to go back to Gabrielle's tent with her. He'd bought her soup because she'd been hungry. She'd accepted for the same reason. She didn't owe him anything. But…how could he not follow her and at least try to get her to talk?

He'd been looking for his angel for so long, needing to find someone who saw what he saw. His parents didn't understand when he told them about his dreams, insisting that everybody saw visions when they slept. But his were different. They weren't like the dreams everyone else had. His used all his senses. He could see everything. Hear everything. Feel and smell whatever was near.

But most of all, he could taste them. And when it came to dreaming of his future, all he could taste was death.

"It doesn't suit you to be so morbid," his mother would say in that well-bred voice of hers. And she was right. It didn't suit him. His natural demeanor was to be happy. But how could he feel upbeat when he had a clock ticking in his ear? So, he'd set out to find an angel to help him understand his dreams. He didn't want to get his hopes up, but he also hoped an angel may be able to help him change his future. Death could surely be cheated if you were warned of its approach?

Gabrielle stopped at the entrance to her tent and turned to face him.

"Thank you for the food," she said, making it clear that this was where their encounter ended. "I have work to do now, while there are still people about."

Cassius looked around. The sun was getting low in the sky and people had that hurried look about them, keen to get back to their families and turn in for the night. He couldn't imagine Gabrielle would have much luck luring any of them in for a reading.

He had a room at the local inn with a bed that was calling to his weary bones. But that was the last place he wanted to go. He just wanted to be wherever Gabrielle was near.

"Cass—"

He never got to find out what it was she was about to say as a loud scream echoed from the end of the row of market stalls, followed by the sound of marching.

"Quickly." Gabrielle grabbed him by the shirt sleeve and dragged him into her tent. "It's another attack. We need to hide!"

"Is it the Guardians?" he asked, having heard a neighboring kingdom had been sending out their soldiers in an effort to build their army and take control of Forte Cadence. Known as Guardians, these soldiers were said to be twice the size of any normal person.

She nodded, the fear in her eyes like a stab in his chest.

He was going to need to protect his heart near her. Gabrielle wasn't possibly the only person in the kingdom who understood him, she was exquisitely beautiful. She had the palest blue eyes he'd ever seen, the sort that could see right through him—which clearly they could. But now wasn't the time to marvel at her appearance. She was frightened and he needed to do everything in his power to keep her safe.

Gabrielle lifted a piece of fabric that revealed a false wall in the back of her tent and gestured for him to follow her to what he could see was a space small enough for a sleeping mat and a few of her possessions.

As much as when he'd first laid eyes on her, he'd wished for such a moment, these weren't quite the circumstances he'd imagined being invited into her bed.

"Search the tents!" a loud voice called.

No wonder Gabrielle was scared. That voice. It was so…deep. Like it belonged more to a giant than a man. Could the rumors about these Guardians be true?

"You hide," he said. "I'm going to stay out here and keep watch."

"It's not safe," she said, crouching down in the corner.

"We both know I'm going to die anyway," he said, wondering if he'd make a different choice had his future been brighter. "May as well go out rescuing a damsel in distress."

"Don't talk like that," she hissed. "We don't know for sure what the future holds. Stay here!"

"It was lovely to meet you, Angel Gabrielle." He went to leave, but she took him by the arm and dragged him back.

"If you leave, then I'm going with you," she said.

"No." He tried to make his voice as firm as he could. "I know how to look after myself."

"And you think I don't?" she said, refusing to let go of his arm.

"Gabrielle." He loosened her grip and brought her hand to his lips. "Please stay here. It's what I want. After what you saw of my future, please don't deny me that."

A single tear wove its way down her cheek, and she reluctantly nodded.

"I'll be careful." He kissed her fingertips then let her hand go. "But whatever happens, I'm glad I met you."

Before she had a chance to respond, he folded back the false wall and stood in the tent, waiting. If these Guardians found it empty, surely, they'd search more thoroughly than if they found him there. With any luck they'd seize him and leave Gabrielle alone.

Crossing his arms to hide his shaking, he held his ground. This was it. This was really it.

He listened to the screams of the stall holders as the Guardians rounded them up, the irony of the situation punching him in the gut. He'd come here because he'd believed he was going to die. Yet it seemed that coming here was going to be the very thing that killed him. Why hadn't he listened to his mother and stayed at home by her side? Then again, at least his death would mean something if it meant he was able to save Gabrielle.

The door to the tent was thrown open and the largest man Cassius had ever seen burst through. He was so tall he was unable to stand up in the tent, which easily accommodated what Cassius had formerly believed to be his own impressive height.

"So, the tonics are real," said Cassius, unable to stop himself from staring at the Guardian before him. The Bay of Laurel was the food bowl kingdom, blessed with bountiful crops and food aplenty. It was said they had herbalists working for them to produce powerful tonics to breed the strongest army the world had ever seen.

He hadn't believed it until now.

"Who else is here?" This Guardian had no interest in discussing tonics with Cassius.

"I work alone," said Cassius. "Would you like your fortune read?" He waved his hand over the covered rock on the table.

The Guardian stooped to get further into the tent and seized Cassius, dragging him outside.

"Kneel," instructed the Guardian. "With your hands behind your head."

Cassius saw that all up and down the rows of market stalls there were people doing the same. His stomach dropped to see the Guardian turn to re-enter Gabrielle's tent.

Daring to get to his feet, Cassius removed a portion of bread he'd hidden in his pocket in the hope of leaving it for Gabrielle to eat later. He threw it onto the middle of the road. The other people lined up saw it and their eyes bulged. Several scurried forward to make a grab for it, wanting one last meal before their inevitable demise.

"Guardian!" Cassius shouted.

The giant man behind him spun around and saw the commotion. Leaving Gabrielle's tent, he marched forward to get everyone back in line.

Cassius quickly ran to the adjacent tent, which appeared to have been found genuinely empty, and knelt with his hands behind his head.

Once the Guardian had everyone back in line, he scowled at Cassius and went into the tent behind him.

"There's nobody in there!" Cassius shouted after him.

"Take me for a fool..." came the muttered response.

"Please, I'm telling the truth," pleaded Cassius, relieved his quick-thinking may have saved the life of an angel.

While he waited for the Guardian to emerge, he watched the chaos around him, feeling somewhat disconnected to it all. Soon, he'd no longer be part of this world. It was strange to think that all of this would continue to go on without him.

Unless his angel could help him in the way that he hoped. Either way, it seemed the time had come for him to find out.

GABRIELLE

THE BEFORE

*G*abrielle remained crouched in her hiding place in the corner of her tent. Her shaking gradually subsided but the sick feeling in her stomach only grew worse with each minute that passed.

Eventually, silence threaded its way through the marketplace and she dared to emerge. Quiet was never a good thing in a place that usually bustled with activity. However, this didn't last long and soon the evening air was punctuated by soft sobs as those who were spared by the Guardians mourned those who weren't.

"Cassius," Gabrielle called, raising her voice as loud as she dared. "Are you here?"

Stepping out of the tent, she looked up and down the deserted row of market stalls, hoping to catch sight of a flash of blond hair.

"Cassius?"

There was nobody there. The Guardians had taken everyone they'd come for, and she had no doubt that would have included Cassius. In previous raids, they'd favored tall, strong males who still had all their teeth. Unfortunately, Cassius ticked all those boxes.

She should have tried harder to insist that he hide with her in the back of the tent. But somehow, he'd convinced her to respect his wishes. After what she'd seen in the vision she'd had of him, she hadn't been able to say no.

Holding her fingertips up to her lips, she remembered the tender way he'd kissed her, and guilt punched her in the gut. She should never have let him go.

Gabrielle left her tent and walked down the dirt road in the dying light of the day, feeling like something deep inside her was also slipping away.

She shook her head, hoping some sense would enter her brain. She only just met Cassius! She hadn't even known he existed a mere number of hours ago. Then again, if she was honest with herself, that didn't feel true either. She'd always known he existed. That a great love would come into her life and win over her entire heart and soul.

She just hadn't known it was Cassius.

A woman stuck her head up over the top of her market stall and peered at Gabrielle. "Have they gone?" she whispered.

"I think so," Gabrielle said sadly.

The woman's eyes flew open. "You think so? Are you crazy? Get back in your tent until you're sure. Hide!"

Gabrielle gave the woman what she hoped was a reassuring smile. "I can no longer hear them. They're gone."

"Oh." The woman stood. "It's you, isn't it? Didn't recognize you for a moment. You're the girl who sees things."

Gabrielle nodded, used to this kind of reaction from strangers.

"They must've gone if you say so." The woman smiled broadly. "Essy! Get out here. The witch says they're gone."

Gabrielle gasped. "Don't call me that. I'm no witch."

She knew only too well what people thought of witches in Forte Cadence. They were women who dabbled in maleficium, otherwise known as harmful magic or evil sorcery. Which couldn't be further from the truth for Gabrielle. Her work was all about shining a light on the truth, not despairing over darkness and death.

The woman narrowed her eyes. "Not everyone around here thinks good of you. Be warned."

The face of the woman with the goat came into Gabrielle's mind and she had to accept this woman was right. Some people thought her intentions were wrong, even if they were the ones whose opinions were misplaced.

"I tell people what they need to hear," Gabrielle said, even though she'd refused to give Cassius his reading. "I tell them the truth."

This seemed to amuse the woman. "Truth! Huh! The truth is that we're all going to starve together while that King of ours stuffs his face with all the food the Valley can provide. Who needs to see that? Not me. Not Essy, either."

Another woman who must be Essy stepped up beside her friend. "You won't be seeing the likes of us in your tent. You're a witch, if you ask me."

"Then it's just as well I didn't ask." Gabrielle gave the women a tight-lipped smile. "Good night, ladies."

She took off down the road, her mind swirling with worries of a different kind now. If people had taken to calling her a witch, it might be time to move on from these markets. Women had been burned or drowned for less than that. Perhaps she'd have been better off letting the Guardians take her, instead of hiding like a coward in the back of her tent while they took the only person to show her an ounce of respect recently.

Because while the woman with the goat had dismissed every word Gabrielle had said, Cassius had hung on them. It was like he already knew his own future before she'd seen it for herself. How was that even possible? Had he visited someone else's tent in another village to have his fortune read?

Gabrielle reached the market square, where the eight rows of stalls converged. It was more of a circle than a square really. A few people had gathered there, with more arriving every minute to see who'd been lost and who'd been spared. The dirt had been kicked up with deep divots left by the Guardians' carriages.

Approaching two middle-aged men deep in conversation, Gabrielle cleared her throat.

"Excuse me, but do you know how many were taken?" she asked.

The men turned to her with incredulous expressions, like they couldn't quite believe she'd spoken to them. Ignoring her, they returned to their conversation.

"Excuse me," she said a little louder this time. "I asked if you know how many were taken?"

The taller of the men let out a sigh and looked at her. "We might have seen the carriage leave. Then again, maybe we didn't."

"What's it worth to ya?" the other man asked, sticking out a hand and rubbing his thumb along the tips of his fingers.

"I don't have any money." Gabrielle took a step back, deciding to ask someone else.

"They took about a dozen," said the taller man, realizing he wasn't going to get anything from her. "That was as many as they could fit in their carriage."

Gabrielle felt a small weight lift from her shoulders. A dozen wasn't a lot given how many thousands were at the market when the Guardians arrived. Perhaps Cassius had just returned to Aria Flats where he said he'd come from.

"Did any of them have blond hair?" she asked.

"Yeah, one of 'em," the other man said. "More like white hair. I only noticed because his eyes were so dark. Not natural if you ask me."

Gabrielle gasped. This man had to be talking about Cassius. The unusual contrast between his hair and eyes had been what Gabrielle had noticed first about him.

"He one of your kind, is he?" the taller man asked. "Seemed like the sort who might be into hocus pocus. Had that look in his eye."

"Not sure why she needs to ask us where he is," the other man said, chuckling. "Could've just looked into her crystal ball and seen for herself."

Gabrielle crossed her arms. It seemed that far more people here knew who she was, even if their faces were new to her.

"Do you know where the Guardians took him?" she asked, ignoring their amusement at her expense.

"Bay of Laurel," the other man said. "He'll be turned into a Guardian. Your boyfriend will be twice the height next time you see him."

Gabrielle stepped away from the men, having all the information out of them that she was going to get. She'd bet they wouldn't find this situation so amusing if someone they cared about had been taken away.

She walked slowly back to her tent, wondering if she really did care about Cassius? The version of herself that she'd seen in her vision, holding his lifeless hand, had seemed to care.

He knew what she'd seen as well. His parting words to her had been proof enough of that.

We both know I'm going to die anyway.

Which meant he'd either met another angel who'd seen a vision of his future, or he'd seen it himself.

Either way, this told Gabrielle one very important thing.

She wasn't the only angel to walk this earth. There was somebody else out there just like her.

Maybe even Cassius himself.

KING VIRTUS

THE BEFORE

*K*ing Virtus let out a large belch, marveling at the length of time he was able to enjoy the deep sound pouring from his mouth. He leaned back in his golden chair and patted his round belly.

The explosion of gas from his gut had left room for a little more food and he reached for the roast meat on his plate and shoved it into his mouth, not bothering to use his fork. The meat was chewy, so he picked up his wine and used that to wash it down.

"Tell cook he roasted the meat too long," he barked at one of his servants before picking a string of flesh from his teeth and flicking it at the heavy burgundy velvet drapes. "The pig was already dead. No need to kill it again."

He laughed at his own joke, turning to his wife to make sure she was enjoying his humor.

Queen Starla smiled, although the wench's pretty eyes remained dead. She didn't think he noticed things like that, but he always did. He wasn't an idiot. Unlike her. She may be pleasing to the eye, but she was also extremely dense. However, she'd given him a son and hope-fully soon she'd provide him with another, so she could stay for now.

Just as long as she didn't try to pass off a daughter on him. Real men didn't sire girls. If she did that, he'd know she really was a wench.

"My meat was cooked fine," she said, further evidence of the insolence he'd noticed growing inside her in place of their second son, which she was taking far too long to produce.

"Well, ours was not." The King raised a brow at her. "Don't tell us that you're protecting cook again?"

"I'm not protecting anyone," the wench said. "My meat was cooked fine."

The King opened his mouth to tell his wife to close hers when young Virtus came running into the room with his nursemaid chasing after him, looking flustered. She made a grab for the boy, but he spun around and kicked her hard in the stomach. The nursemaid let out a groan.

"Let me go!" Young Virtus squealed.

The nursemaid tightened her hold.

"Let the boy go," King Virtus boomed, stretching out his arms. "Are you deaf? He wants to come to his father."

His son was released immediately and ran to the wench instead.

"Go to your father," she whispered in his ear, trying to prise him off her lap.

"Don't want to," the boy whimpered, burying his face in his mother's chest.

The King stood from his chair and stalked over to his son, his silk slippers sliding on the marble floor.

"You are Virtus the boy right now," he said, pointing at the boy. "But one day, you are to be King Virtus. You cannot spend your days sniveling like a pathetic little girl. Be a man! Be strong and powerful."

For some reason, the boy didn't respond to this moving speech and remained with his face hidden in his mother's ample bosom.

"You're scaring him," the wench said. "He'll come to you when he's ready."

"No." King Virtus kept his voice level. "He'll come to his father when his father says so."

The boy responded to this by holding onto his disobedient mother more tightly. She was in on this act of heresy, it was obvious.

King Virtus bent down and put his strong hands on his son, pulling him away from the wench and pinning him in his arms. The boy squirmed in the same way he'd done with his nursemaid. But being a man, the King was far smarter than the nursemaid and managed to secure the boy's feet before he could deliver another kick.

"Make him sit still," the King directed the wench. "Or you can spend a night in the dungeon thinking about how you can get our son to behave."

Queen Starla leaped from her chair and squatted down in front of them.

"Virtus," she cooed. There was a time when she'd used that very same name with equal tenderness, only it had been directed at him. It seemed that once he'd made her Queen and she had what she wanted, her true feelings had been revealed. "If you stay still for your father, I'll take you to the garden to play with the hens."

The boy instantly ceased his protestations and sat still. There was nothing in this kingdom he loved more than those godforsaken hens. If you asked King Virtus, the only good thing about those pathetic feathered creatures was eating them.

"You come from a long line of strong kings called Virtus," the King told his son.

"I know this story," the boy whispered defiantly.

"*We,*" the King corrected. "Not I. As future King, you must learn to speak of yourself in the plural, for you are speaking for the entire Kingdom, such is the sacrifice we make."

The boy nodded, although King Virtus was entirely uncertain if he understood.

"Our father was Virtus," he continued. "And his father before him, and his father before him."

"*We* know," the boy replied, showing that while defiant, he was indeed clever enough to understand what he was being told.

"Good," the King said. "You must know the story well. Because one day, you will grow up and become King Virtus and you will rule over

Forte Cadence, just like we do today. Then you will have a son and you will call him Virtus. He will sit on your lap just like you are on our lap now, and you will tell him this same story. Then he will grow up and become King. And so it will go on."

"Mother said *we* might have a girl baby one day," said the boy. "And that she will be Queen instead."

King Virtus gasped, unable to hide his disgust with the wench for spreading such hateful thoughts. It was true that his great-great-great-grandfather had changed the law of succession so the first-born child would be heir, no matter their gender. That particular King Virtus had a daughter for a first-born who he claimed was also the most intelligent of his children. The story was as ludicrous as it was frustrating. Thankfully the ridiculous law had never had to be enacted as her younger brother was heroic enough to ensure she never survived to be Queen. Virtus's ancestors had then all gone on to be manly enough to produce a boy first. (Except for his grandfather, although his daughter had most fortunately died suddenly in her sleep, so she didn't count.)

"You will have a son, not a daughter," King Virtus said firmly. "You will call him Virtus. And he will rule not just our kingdom, but all the kingdoms in the world."

"But mother said—"

"Enough, Virtus." The wench smiled nervously. "Your father doesn't want to hear that."

"No, we'd like to hear what your mother had to say." King Virtus jostled his son on his knee. "Tell us."

The boy glanced across at his mother who'd begun to shake. She crossed her arms and a single tear rolled down her cheek, proving how weak she really was.

Young Virtus swallowed and looked back at his father. "Mother said our kingdom is falling. She said the Guardians are taking our strongest fighters, and that when they attack we'll have no hope. We'll belong to The Bay of Laurel soon."

"Did she now?" The King settled his son back on his feet and patted him affectionately on his arm. There was hope for this boy yet. "That's very interesting. What else did she have to say?"

His son beamed, pleased to have his father's approval. "She said you're eating all the starving people's food and that's why you're so fat."

King Virtus stood, pushing his son aside to grab the wench by her traitorous throat. He shoved her against the table and tightened his grip on her.

"Please," she gasped as she was forced backward until she was lying across the remains of the meal they'd just shared. "I could be with child."

He looked down at her delicate waistline and laughed. "There's nothing in there. Not for lack of trying on our behalf either. You're as useless as you are stupid."

He had what he needed from this wench. He had his son. There'd be other wenches able to provide him with what he wanted. And they'd be far more compliant than this one had been recently.

As he choked the last of the wasted air from her lungs, he looked across at young Virtus and saw something that made his heart swell with pride.

His son was smiling.

He was going to make a wonderful king.

CASSIUS

THE BEFORE

assius sat in the back of the Guardians' carriage with his knees tucked up under his chin, wincing every time the wheels hit a bump. There were nine others crammed in with him. Seven males, two females. Most of them a similar age to Cassius.

The carriage lurched as it dipped into a divot in the road and Cassius was thrown against the man beside him. He didn't apologize, having given up on that after the first hundred times it happened.

Once the carriage steadied itself, Cassius shuffled back an inch, trying to regain the only personal space available. It felt like this journey was never going to end. It wasn't like he wasn't used to traveling either. He'd been all over Forte Cadence in his search to find his angel. But having never left the kingdom before, he'd had no idea just how far away The Bay of Laurel was. It was like they were being taken to the other end of the Earth.

The carriage was a large, windowless wooden box being pulled by four strong mules. A prison cell on wheels, with the doors at the rear kept firmly bolted. There was a bucket at one end for *emergencies*, and every few hours the Guardians stopped and let them out for a few precious moments, giving them cornbread and a few sips of water before being corralled back inside.

The Guardians themselves sat behind the mules, controlling them with long leather reins. Occasionally they could be heard talking to each other but Cassius could never quite make out what they were saying.

A woman across from Cassius let out a sob, and the man beside her put his arm around her shoulders. She buried her face in his chest and allowed her tears to fall. The man wrapped her in one of the blankets they'd been supplied with. Cassius remained quiet, wondering what kind of life any of these people had that might have been worth holding onto in a kingdom that was slowly running out of food.

But Cassius wasn't foolish enough to express these thoughts out loud. Because there was nothing any of them could do to change what was happening to them. The Guardians were twice their size, and from what Cassius had seen of the landscape so far, there was nowhere to run. What was the point in gaining your freedom only to die in a dusty field?

Gabrielle's sweet face popped into Cassius's mind, reminding him that maybe he had a life worth holding onto. Being captured by the Guardians had torn him away from the one person he'd spent his life searching for, just as he'd found her. Although, staying with Gabrielle wasn't exactly a solid plan either, given the future he'd seen play out with her in his dreams.

"I think we're nearly there," Cassius said.

Nobody answered, but just because someone doesn't offer you a reply doesn't mean they didn't hear you.

"Can you feel it?" he asked the man beside him. "I think we're going over a bridge."

"And I think you should keep quiet," one of the other men grumbled.

"Leave him," said the woman who'd been crying. She sat up straight and tilted her head. "I think he's right. It does feel different."

Cassius smiled. This was the closest he'd come to having a conversation in the time they'd been locked in here together. Even if it was bordering on becoming an argument, he'd take it. He'd been unaware of how lonely it was possible to become, even when he wasn't by himself. It seems loneliness can't be cured by people, but rather the right people.

"The ground's flattening out now." He tilted his head, using all his senses. "And we no longer have dust creeping through the cracks in the walls. Can you smell the air? It feels fresher."

"Why are you in such a hurry to get there?" a man growled. "They'll probably kill us. Are you in a rush to die?"

Cassius shook his head, knowing he wouldn't be dying at the Guardians' hands, but unable to explain that in a way that would make sense to anyone here.

"They didn't come all the way to the market to get us, then bring us all the way back to their kingdom to kill us," he said. "They need us for something."

"Well, I'm not helping them with anything," one of the other men said. "Not unless they agree to take me home. I have a son I need to get back to."

Cassius nodded, feeling sorry for him. It's one thing to miss an angel you'd only just met, but another altogether to miss a child you'd brought into the world.

The carriage carried on its journey, practically gliding now, and a sense of anticipation built as the people began to believe what he'd said.

They must be nearly there.

The mules slowed, and the carriage came to an abrupt stop.

One of Cassius's companions moved the two females to the rear of the carriage. Cassius readied himself for a fight, even though he knew it was useless. The Guardians had overpowered all of them with such ease at the markets. Whatever it was they had planned for them, there was no doubt they'd succeed. He was grateful that so far, nobody had been hurt. While the Guardians had been firm, they'd also been surprisingly gentle.

The doors were thrown open with a bang and light poured into the carriage. Cassius blinked at what he saw, certain he must be imagining it. Instead of the stern Guardians who'd captured them waiting on the other side, there was another group of much friendlier looking

Guardians with wide smiles and bowls of food in their hands. These ones were just as tall and layered with muscle, but they seemed softer somehow. Some were even female, which surprised Cassius.

"Welcome," the Guardians chorused. "We're so happy to have you here."

Nobody said a word in response, afraid they might say the wrong thing. Cassius wasn't even sure the food they held was for them. Perhaps they'd arrived at the wrong time and had interrupted their evening meal?

"Please, come out of the carriage," one of the women said. "You must be so tired after the journey. We've prepared food and tonic for you in the tavern."

Cassius was the first to climb out with his stomach growling. The bowl of soup he'd eaten with Gabrielle felt like an eternity ago. The cornbread he'd been given had barely touched the sides of his belly.

As his feet made contact with the soft grass, his eyes widened and he struggled to decide what to look at first. The Bay of Laurel was so...lush. The carriage had pulled up outside a long building made from timber that must be the tavern the woman had mentioned. Around it sat little huts that seemed to be homes, with children playing happily outside their doors. There was a large area of grass off to the side where Guardians were lifting heavy objects and stretching their superhuman frames. In the distance, he could see a stone castle. It was likely the same size as King Virtus's but given it was much closer it seemed twice as large.

But the thing that had Cassius most surprised were the gardens that surrounded all these structures. Food was growing everywhere he looked. He could see fields of corn and peppers alongside orchards bursting with apples and pears. There was even an herb garden made up of a mosaic of every shade of green he could imagine. He'd never seen so much food all at once and he longed for Gabrielle to be by his side so she could see it too.

Cassius entered the tavern alongside his reluctant companions. Cups were lined up on a long, wooden table and he took the closest one, raising it to his lips and wincing at the bitter taste of the tonic.

The others were more hesitant, waiting to see if Cassius survived before they dared to sample their own. But as Cassius had explained, he didn't believe the Guardians had any intention to hurt them. They'd had plenty of opportunity to do that and hadn't.

"It's good," said Cassius with a nod. "I mean, it tastes terrible, but I feel more energetic already. Maybe it will make us grow taller."

One by one, the others gathered their courage and drank their tonics.

"You won't grow taller," said one of the female Guardians. "But we can add some muscle to those skinny bones."

Cassius nodded as he took in this woman. She had blonde hair pulled into a braid, with one curl at the front that had escaped. She was one of the shortest Guardians, which didn't say much as Cassius still only came up to her shoulders. About a decade older than him, she had a kind face and a warm smile.

She nodded at him. "Welcome to The Bay of Laurel."

He stepped closer and lowered his voice. "Why are we here? What's happening? Why were we kidnapped?"

The woman narrowed her eyes, seeming surprised by his question. "What do you mean? You were rescued, not kidnapped."

Cassius wasn't sure that being taken against your will is the same thing as being rescued but he didn't argue the point and risk upsetting her.

"What are you going to do with us?" he asked.

Again, she seemed confused. "We're going to feed you and make you strong. Then if you wish to stay, you can become part of our army."

"And if we don't wish to stay?" he asked.

The Guardian looked surprised. "Nobody's ever chosen not to stay. I'm not sure."

"Nobody?" Cassius tilted his head.

"You'll see." She smiled at him. "You won't want to leave us either."

"I'll be leaving you," grumbled Cassius's companion who needed to get back to his son. "You took me from my family. They need me."

The Guardian didn't seem worried by this. "You'll stay too. Everyone does."

Cassius moved across to the table where the bowls of food had been placed, his mouth watering as he was passed a large meal. He decided that if the Guardians had taken him a day earlier it was very possible he might have chosen to stay in this place. A life in an abundant kingdom with a permanently full belly didn't seem so bad. Especially when compared to the alternative he'd seen in his dreams.

But they hadn't taken him a day earlier. He'd found his angel now. And no matter what direction his life went, their paths were destined to cross again.

Which meant this Guardian with the kind smile was going to find out what happened when someone decided not to stay. Because it wasn't so much that Cassius couldn't stay, but more that the universe had already decided that he wouldn't.

GABRIELLE

THE BEFORE

*G*abrielle moved through the days after Cassius disappeared in a blur built on both sadness and fatigue. Her tent at the market had never been busier. Since this last visit from the Guardians, it seemed everyone wanted to know their future. Would they be taken too? Or would their son? Their husband? Their sister?

This put Gabrielle in an extremely difficult position. She needed to earn money to get her share of the dwindling food supplies in the kingdom but having to carefully deliver news of hopeless futures to customer after customer was extremely draining. And that wasn't because she foresaw kidnappings in their future. Instead, she saw hunger. Desperation. Homelessness. And grief. And all of it taking place right here. She longed for someone to visit who was actually destined to be taken. Maybe then she could catch a glimpse into the life Cassius had been taken to.

Gabrielle woke early one morning, feeling unusually cold. She pulled her blanket up to her chin, putting off having to climb out of her bed at the back of her tent. Her clothes were starting to hang loosely on her, a result of more water being added to the soup, along with smaller portions of everything else. Was it like this in other parts of Forte Cadence, or just the Valley of the Blessed? Cassius had come from Aria Flats and he seemed in better health than her. At the moment anyway.

That was another thing she wondered about. Why had she been shown a vision of Cassius's death so clearly if she was never going to see him again? It couldn't possibly come true now that he'd been taken. Perhaps in life something so unexpected could happen that it could throw off the course of your future permanently. Just because she'd never seen this happen before didn't mean it wasn't possible. If only her mother were here to ask. Had she encountered anything like this? But like everything in life these days, it seemed Gabrielle was left to figure out this mystery for herself.

"Hello?" came a female voice at the door to her tent. "Is anyone here?"

"I'm not open yet," she called out. "Come back later."

"Please," the woman begged, desperation clear in her tone.

Gabrielle let out a sigh and threw off her blanket. Maybe if she did this reading quickly, she could buy herself a cup of hot tea.

"Wait there," she said. "I need a moment to prepare."

"Thank you."

With no need to dress given Gabrielle always slept in her clothes, she quickly made herself presentable by running a comb through her curls and used the bowl of water she kept by her bed to splash her face. That would have to do for now. She quickly set up her table in the main room of her small tent, then opened the flap.

A young woman stood with her arms crossed against the cold morning, and Gabrielle ushered her inside.

"Two copper coins and the future is yours," said Gabrielle. She'd dropped her price recently, not due to lack of customers but rather an overload of guilt. These people had so little and it was clear they were starving. She couldn't take any more than she needed. There may come a time when one copper coin would have to be enough.

"I have no money," the woman said, once inside the tent.

"What do you have then?" Gabrielle asked, quite used to this situation.

The woman removed a woollen shawl from her shoulders and held it out. "You may have this. Please, I need to know my future."

Gabrielle hesitated to take the shawl. It looked warm, but this woman seemed to need it more than she did. The dress she wore underneath was hardly any protection from this weather. After a pause, Gabrielle took it, folded it and put it on the table beside her covered rock. She'd wait to see the woman's future before deciding if she'd accept it or not. It was bad business practice, but she needed to be able to live with herself as well as the others around her.

"Sit down," she told the woman, taking a seat and placing her hands on either side of the stone. "Give me your hands."

The woman sat and gave Gabrielle her hands. They remained quiet for several minutes while Gabrielle waited for the visions to arrive.

Eventually, she was shown an image of this woman in a large room with high timber rafters that criss-crossed beneath a golden dome. It was a room Gabrielle wasn't at all familiar with. There were lines of men and women in robes with their heads shaved bald. The woman sitting before her was one of them. The robed people were chanting something over and over, and a man with a sword stood at the front of the room with a terrible scowl on his face.

"What do you see?" the woman asked, unable to remain quiet. "Will I live?"

"Shh," Gabrielle hushed, trying her best to make sense of this image before she spoke. In the hundreds of readings she'd done before, she'd never seen anything like this. Could this be The Bay of Laurel? Is this what the Guardians were taking the people for? To shave their heads and line them up to call to their gods?

"What is it?" the woman asked again.

The vision faded and Gabrielle let go of the woman's hands, trying to decide what to say.

"You'll survive this famine," she said. "I saw your face. You were older than you are today. You were with others who also looked healthy and you had a solid roof over your heads."

The woman narrowed her eyes at Gabrielle's vagueness. "What about my husband? My son? Was I with them?"

Gabrielle wasn't sure who the other robed people were in her vision, but she was certain they weren't this woman's family. She'd felt a disconnect between them, like they hadn't known each other at all despite their common circumstances.

She pushed the shawl back to the woman. "That's all I can tell you. Please, take this. I have enough warmth."

What she'd told her was true. The people she'd seen looked physically healthy aside from their lack of hair. They were thin but not starving as they were now. And their robes were warm. But there was also a deep sadness emanating from them. A sadness that made it impossible for Gabrielle to take anything from this woman while she still had things to hold onto. This woman would survive. But her future was arguably one that was worse than death.

Could this be where Cassius was sent? In her vision of him, he'd had hair. Everything was different. Unless her earlier theory was correct and his kidnapping had changed the course of where he was headed in life.

The woman took back her shawl, wrapping it around the hunch of her disappointed shoulders. She was no fool. If Gabrielle had foreseen a happy future, why then had she returned her payment?

Gabrielle stood and held out a hand to the door. "You'll live to an old age. That's good news in these times."

A sob escaped the woman's lips and she nodded, taking this news in the same way as if Gabrielle had told her she was going to die. "If I bring you my son, will you read for him?"

Gabrielle found herself nodding. "I can't guarantee that I'll see anything. Children can be difficult to read."

This wasn't strictly true. It was more that Gabrielle didn't like to frighten children if all she saw was black. And one thing she never did was lie to her customers. That would go against everything she stood for.

"Thank you." The woman left the tent and Gabrielle slumped in her chair. Would she ever see a happy future again? Perhaps it was time to visit King Virtus herself and beg for change. If only that wasn't a sure path to death. He'd never listen to a *witch* like herself. She'd be lucky if he let her leave alive.

A young man's face appeared at the entrance to her tent and Gabrielle's head snapped up. She was always extra cautious when a man came to her. Not only was it less common for men to want their futures read, but she had to guard herself from physical threat. Thankfully, this man had a friendly smile on his dirt-stained face.

"Come in," Gabrielle said. "Two coins and your future is yours."

The man placed two coins on the table and Gabrielle slipped them into her pocket, surprised not to have had to barter with him.

"Put your hands in mine," she instructed, already dreading what she was going to see, especially after her last confusing vision.

This man's future came quickly, firing into the front of her mind and she let out a gasp. She saw the man in a field, a castle looming in the background. The man was picking ears of corn and placing them in a basket while a fat rabbit hopped past. There were others in the cornfield, all plump and humming to themselves as they worked.

"Will I be taken?" The man's long, dark hair fell into his eye, but he didn't break his hold on her to push it out of the way.

Gabrielle turned her words over in her head, certain she knew what this vision meant.

"I see happiness in your future," she said. "You're surrounded by friends. You have work to keep you busy. And plenty of food to fill your belly."

The man's eyes narrowed in suspicion and he leaned forward. "You must be a fraud. Nobody has that future here."

Gabrielle swallowed. "Your future won't be here. You'll be taken by the Guardians."

The man let go of her hands, his face filled with horror. "But you said—"

"That you'll be happy," she finished. "And you will be. The Guardians can offer you a life that you can't hope to have here. And I think you should take it."

CASSIUS

THE BEFORE

assius ran until his legs ached. He lifted iron balls until his arms screamed in pain. And he drank tonics until the bitter taste almost became sweet.

The female Guardian had been right. He wasn't growing any taller, but it was adding muscle to his skinny bones. Not that he was actually sure bones could be skinny, although he knew what she meant. Every day he felt stronger. Life was easier to enjoy with a healthy body and mind.

The only thing that could make it any better would be to have Gabrielle by his side. Although, part of him was apprehensive about that wish. He hadn't had a single dream about dying since he'd arrived here. Had this fork in the path of his future set him on another course?

He climbed into his soft bed in the small wooden hut he'd been assigned to. He shared the space with Gregor, the man who was so upset to have been taken away from his son. He'd stopped saying that after a while, instead whispering at night as he asked Cassius if he thought it was possible to bring his son here.

Cassius had no answer to that. He only had more questions of his own. But there was one that plagued his mind most of all.

Would he still choose this path of a healthy body and mind if it meant never seeing Gabrielle again? Because while he'd only spent the shortest amount of time with her, he knew without hesitation they were meant to be together.

He'd had his fair share of female attention over the years, but nobody had spoken to his soul in the same way as his angel. It seemed impossible that their paths would fail to cross again despite the many miles that lay between here and Forte Cadence.

As the Guardians brought more carriages of starving people into The Bay of Laurel, Cassius heard more stories about the plight of the people of Forte Cadence. Life was getting harder, and food was becoming even more scarce. He asked them if they'd seen the girl in the tent who saw the future and they shook their heads firmly, saying they didn't believe in such things.

Which meant that while Cassius felt strong and satisfied with his new life, he also felt very alone.

Gregor let out an enormous snore and Cassius decided to go outside for a while and take in some fresh air. There was no chance he was going to fall asleep with that racket inside.

He wandered away from the Guardians' village and found himself walking to the herb garden beside the tavern where they came to take their tonics each day. It was peaceful here and filled with rosemary, basil, coriander and oregano, making him wonder why he hadn't explored this peaceful garden earlier.

He let his fingertips brush over the green leaves in the moonlight, releasing a variety of scents. Some spicy, some fresh and others sharp and complex. He drew them into his lungs, wishing he knew all their names. If only the woman who sold soup at Gabrielle's market had access to some of these, she could boost the health of the people of Forte Cadence while creating some delicious flavors.

He understood now what the Guardian had meant when she said they were rescuing the people from Forte Cadence, not kidnapping them. The Bay of Laurel had plenty of food to share and there was no way any of these starving people would have come willingly, such was the mistrust between the kingdoms.

It would be a blessing if King Virtus were overthrown by an army of Guardians. Cassius would happily fight for his new kingdom. As long as the people of Forte Cadence came to no harm, of course. They were innocent in this war.

He reached for a plant variety he hadn't seen before and crouched down to study it. It had rounded leaves and a strong, sharp smell.

"What's your name?" he asked it.

A soft laugh came from behind him. "Mint."

He turned and saw a woman. Not a Guardian. This woman had dark hair and was of regular height.

His cheeks pinked to have been caught talking to a bush, but somehow he didn't think this woman was the sort to think twice about something like that.

"Mint helps with sleep, if that's what you're having trouble with." The woman smiled at him. "I could make you a tonic, if you like?"

"Are you the herbalist?" he asked, his eyes widening. He'd heard about the woman who worked in the kitchen adjoining the tavern, following an ancient book of recipes that had been recorded by her ancestors. Somehow, he hadn't expected her to look quite so *ordinary*.

He squinted at her in the dim light, wishing he could get a better look at her. She had brown hair, lines crinkling around her eyes and a friendly smile. She reminded him a little of his own mother back home.

"I'm Sage." The woman nodded. "And yes, I'm the herbalist. I've been waiting for you."

Cassius's hand flew to his chest. "Me?"

"Yes, you." Sage smiled in such a way it was impossible not to trust her. "Come inside and I'll make you a hot tonic and explain."

Cassius followed her into a small house behind the herb garden. It never occurred to him that the herbalist would live in the same place she worked.

There were several candles burning on a large wooden table in the center of a homely kitchen. Sage held her finger to her lips as he took his seat.

"We need to keep our voices down," she whispered as she went to a stove and poured some steaming liquid into a mug, like she'd known he was coming. "My young daughter, Ariel, is asleep."

"You're very trusting," he said, accepting the mug and cradling it between his hands. "Where I come from, nobody would let a strange man into their house. Especially with their daughter asleep."

"But you're not a strange man." Sage slid into a chair across from him. "You're an angel."

It was fortunate that Cassius hadn't lifted the mug to his lips as he'd have dropped it immediately.

"Don't look so shocked." A soft laugh tinkled from her lips. "In time, you'll come to recognize your own kind. Have you never met an angel before?"

"That depends on what you mean," he said.

"I'm not talking about creatures with wings, flying down from the clouds." Sage smiled warmly. "But I think you knew that already. I'm talking about humans who know things other humans don't. Things that can't be explained."

"In that case, I've only met the one angel." Gabrielle's beautiful face floated into his mind.

"Drink your tonic." Sage nodded at his mug. "It'll calm your nerves."

"What do you know about me?" Cassius took a sip of tonic and let out a sigh as it slipped down his throat. This drink lacked the bitterness of his daily tonic and he felt immediately calmer, despite what he'd just been told.

Sage shook her head. "I don't know anything about you, really. But I've been dreaming of an angel coming to me for help. As soon as I saw you, I knew it was you."

"But I didn't come here looking for help," Cassius said. "I couldn't sleep. I went for a walk and found myself in your garden."

"Found yourself?" Sage asked. "Why did you come here at the exact moment I felt a calling to step out and look for you?"

He shrugged. It was true he'd felt a pull toward Sage's garden. Was there some help from her that he hadn't known he needed?

"You're confused about your future," she said, more as a statement than a question. "Life isn't turning out the way you thought it would."

He nodded, although anyone could have told him that. It's obvious he was one of those taken from Forte Cadence. How could any of them have predicted this kind of life for themselves?

"Your dreams are real," she said solemnly. "You see your destiny and there's no path you can take that will change it."

Cassius shook his head. "You don't understand. In the future that I see, I'm dying. And an angel sits beside my bed, holding my hand."

Sage nodded. "And is this the angel you say you've met?"

"Yes," he said. "I think so. I've never seen her face in my dreams. I've just felt her there beside me. But, anyway, the only reason I met her is because of the dream. If I'd never dreamed of her, I'd never have gone looking for her."

This made Sage laugh. She put her hand to her mouth to stifle it, glancing toward the room where her daughter slept. "You would always have gone looking for your angel, whether you dreamed of her or not. Your life would never have felt whole without her."

"You don't understand." He took another sip of the warm tonic, trying to figure out how to explain it. "I found her, but then I was taken away. Are you saying I should leave here to find her again?"

"I have no idea." Sage's face turned serious in the flickering light. "All I know is that there will come a time when you'll lie in a bed dying, and your angel will hold your hand. It doesn't matter whether you seek her out or not."

Cassius sat back in his chair and let out a long breath. He hadn't escaped his premature death by his future heading in an unexpected direction. But how was it possible that he'd die with Gabrielle by his side when he was in one kingdom and she was far away in the next?

"Your angel is a very important angel," Sage said. "Have you realized that yet?"

Cassius nodded. He'd known that the first moment he'd seen her.

"She's going to change the world." Sage sipped on her own tonic as she looked into the darkness outside her window. "She's going to save many lives. But it will be at her own expense. Which means she'll need to be brave. Perhaps having you in her life will show her how to do that?"

"But if what you say is true, our future is set in stone. It doesn't matter if my angel is a lion or a mouse. Her outcome in life will still be the same."

"I didn't say that." Sage fixed her gaze on him. "There's plenty in your life that you can shape and change. But the things an angel is shown in a vision are difficult to change. Maybe even impossible."

Taking a sip of his tonic, Cassius absorbed the meaning of these words along with the soothing liquid. He'd been so focussed on considering the impact Gabrielle would have on his life, he hadn't really thought about the impact he might have on hers.

"Not every love story has the same kind of happy ending." Sage smiled warmly at Cassius. "In fact, it's cute that you thought there would be anything ordinary about your story at all."

He grinned at her teasing. "I still don't know if I should stay here or go and look for her."

"Whatever you do, it will be the right decision." Sage stood, indicating their conversation was over. "You're exactly where you're meant to be right now. All of us are."

Cassius drank the last of his tonic and allowed Sage to usher him out the door. She'd given him a lot to think about.

He walked back through the garden, seeing Gabrielle everywhere he looked. She was in the beauty of the moon. The sweetness of the herbs. The comfort of the warm night air.

If what Sage said was true, seeing Gabrielle again was in his future. As long as he made the right decision, which Sage seemed certain he would.

There was only one problem with that. The pressure of making the right choice left him feeling unable to make any choice at all.

GABRIELLE

THE BEFORE

Gabrielle trudged along the rocky path that led directly up Mount Allegro, heading toward the forest that ringed the King's castle. She was still unsure why she'd woken up thinking this was a good idea. Well, not a good idea exactly. But something that she needed to do.

The two readings she'd provided recently had confused her greatly, and both for very different reasons.

The vision of the man having a happy life in The Bay of Laurel had brought home just how desperate things had become in this kingdom. If being kidnapped was the best thing that could happen to you, then clearly something was very wrong. King Virtus needed to open his eyes and see for himself what was happening before it was too late.

Then there was the vision of the woman chanting. That one had disturbed her because the more she'd thought about it, the more she'd become certain the room she'd seen was the King's arena. And as she walked up the rocky hill now, this was only being confirmed even more. She could see the arena perched on top of the mountain with its oval-domed, golden roof catching the light and sending colorful rays of light bouncing across the grass. This arena was where the King's army trained and was the jewel of Forte Cadence.

It also had to be the scene of the misery Gabrielle had seen in her vision. There was no other building in the kingdom that had the same opulence. By why had that woman been there with her long robes and shaved head, chanting alongside so many others? It had been one of the strangest things Gabrielle had ever come across and beyond anything she was capable of imagining.

She stumbled on a rock and pressed on with her climb, grateful she hadn't twisted her ankle. She was almost at the top now and it had taken her the best part of the day. Turning back would take just as long and be impossible in the dark.

Would the King even talk to her? And if he did, would he listen to what she had to say? She knew she had to be careful. If she mentioned her visions, she'd be labeled a witch and thrown into one of the palace's notorious dungeons. But there really was no choice. She couldn't sit by and watch everyone around her die of starvation. Or potentially worse—be locked in the King's arena and forced to chant. She could feel the sadness of the people emanating off them in that vision. They were completely devoid of hope.

Perhaps she'd be better off trying to talk to Queen Starla. She was known to be far kinder than her husband. Although, she had no real power so there was no use in that. If Gabrielle was going to have any impact on changing things for the better, she needed to talk to the King himself. There was also a rumor floating around the kingdom that the Queen was unwell. Nobody had seen her in days, not even the palace staff. It seemed the King was Gabrielle's only option.

The palace loomed into sight behind the arena. Its stone walls were dark and gloomy, a stark contrast to the glittering arena. Gabrielle began to lose her nerve and almost turned around. But one thought kept her legs moving.

Cassius.

As much as she didn't want to believe the vision she'd had of him, she did. And she couldn't possibly live to see him die if King Virtus locked her in his dungeon and left her to rot. So, in some strange way, he was with her now, giving her the strength she needed to keep walking.

She made her way down the wide path to the palace gates and two guards stalked forward to speak to her.

"What's your business here?" the tall one asked.

"I wish to talk to the King." Gabrielle pulled back her shoulders and did her best to look sure of herself.

The two guards looked at each other and laughed.

"Take me to him," said Gabrielle. "I have an important message."

"Very well," said the tall guard. "But first I have to check you for weapons. It's procedure."

Gabrielle held out her arms and lifted her chin, grimacing as the guard felt down her body, taking far longer than was necessary. When the inspection was over, the guard elbowed his partner in the ribs and let out a deep chuckle.

"Sorry, Miss. Still can't let you in," he said. "But thanks for the inspection. Most enjoyable."

"You have to let me in!" Gabrielle felt ill at the invasion but was determined to press on. "The future of the kingdom depends on the information I have to give the King. Tell him that, then see if he'll deny me an audience."

The tall guard's brows shot up. "What could a skinny girl like you possibly know that would change the future of our kingdom?"

Gabrielle sighed, accepting she was going to need to reveal her abilities in order to get anyone to listen to what she had to say. Even if it meant risking the dungeon. There was more at stake here than her own future.

"Give me your hand," she said, putting out her own.

The guard licked his lips and chuckled. "Want another inspection, do you?"

"Just give it to me." Gabrielle wriggled her fingers and waited. "I'll tell you something about yourself that will convince you I know things about the future."

The guard took her hand and Gabrielle closed her eyes to concentrate. Instantly, her soul was flooded with darkness and she tried to pull back, but the guard held her tightly.

She saw an older version of the guard clutching a dagger with a blade that had been inscribed with intricate patterns. At his feet was a terrified man on his knees begging for his life, while an attractive red-headed woman cowered in the corner of the room, half-naked and clutching a sheet to her chest.

The guard let go of her hand and the vision vanished. Gabrielle drew in a deep breath, trying to recover from what she'd just seen.

"Well?" said the guard, still chuckling. "What do you have to tell me?"

"You have a wife," said Gabrielle, treading carefully, especially now that she knew how dangerous this man was. "She has red hair and a nose that points up at the tip. She's very pretty. Younger than you and she has a delicate smattering of freckles across her cheeks."

This wiped the smile from the guard's face. "You've been following me, have you? Anyone could know what my woman looks like if they were keeping a watch on me."

The shorter of the guards, who had been yet to speak, bristled at these words, as if expecting trouble. This set Gabrielle further on edge. She had to handle this exactly right.

"You also own a dagger," said Gabrielle. "It's not an ordinary knife, but one that's been passed down to you over generations."

This last part was a pure guess, but it seemed unlikely a guard being paid by the King would be able to afford a dagger like the one she'd seen in her vision.

"Go on," said the guard.

"It has patterns inscribed in the blade," said Gabrielle. "You carry it under your clothes."

This time, she was banking on the slight bulge that she could see at his hip, just above his belt, being the knife she'd seen in her vision.

"You said you were going to tell me my future," the guard growled, clearly not liking how accurate she'd been so far.

"There will come a time when you see something that makes you very angry with a young man with long, black hair and fair skin," said Gabrielle. "And you'll pull your dagger from your belt to take this man's life. But you won't. Because when it happens, you'll think of this exact moment. And you'll remember that you're a good person, not a murderer. You'll let the young man live."

"Sounds like he deserves to die," the guard grumbled.

Gabrielle shook her head. She had no way of knowing how her vision would turn out, and from the awful feeling it gave her when she saw it, she strongly suspected the young man was not destined to live. But she had to try to save his life if she could. Maybe she could shape the future with this one simple act. Was that why she'd felt compelled to visit the palace—not because she was meant to warn the King, but because she was supposed to save this man's life?

"If you kill him, you'll bring terrible fortune upon yourself," said Gabrielle. "If you let him live, you'll experience great riches."

This was the closest Gabrielle had ever come to telling a lie in one of her readings. But technically it wasn't a lie at all. Murdering someone in cold blood rarely brought about good luck. And there are great riches in going to bed at night with a clear conscience.

"Let me set you straight," the guard growled. "If what you said ever comes about, I'll not only kill the man, I'll kill my wife as well."

"Right, that's enough now," said the shorter guard. "Be on your way."

"No." The tall guard gripped Gabrielle roughly by the arm and dragged her through the palace gates. "This one needs an audience with the King."

Gabrielle's heart both soared and sank. When she'd tried to convince him to let her in, she hadn't expected to be treated like this.

"Let her go!" The shorter guard ran after them. "Come on, there's no need for this. She's only a kid. His Majesty doesn't need to know anything about her."

The tall guard brought Gabrielle to an abrupt stop and brought his face right in front of hers. "What do you reckon, eh? Do you still want to see the King? Because something tells me he's going to have a lot of fun with the likes of you?"

"Let her go," the other guard pleaded. Gabrielle looked across at him and saw kindness in his eyes. She had to be brave. Returning to the market wasn't going to fix anything. This may not fix anything either.

But she had to try. Too many people had been doing nothing for too long. Especially the King.

"Then I'll give her a choice," the tall guard sneered. "Since she's so keen on talking about the future, let her choose her own."

"What's my choice?" Gabrielle choked out.

"I'll either take you to the King," he said. "Or you can spend the night with me."

"Go with Jaff," the shorter guard said urgently.

This spoke volumes in itself, given how much he seemed to fear the man who had such a tight grip on her. If the King were even worse than this brute, she was surely in grave danger.

"Take me to King Virtus," she said, trying to sound courageous. That was who she'd come to speak to. She couldn't back out now.

"You can't help some people," the shorter guard muttered, turning back to the gate.

"Pity," said Jaff, hauling her up the path toward the castle. "I'd have made you a very happy girl."

Gabrielle thought of Cassius as she stumbled along. He'd had so much courage when the Guardians came to the market.

Now, it was her turn. No more cowering in the back of her tent, hiding from the dangers of the world.

It was time to stand up.

CASSIUS

THE BEFORE

*C*assius crawled into his bed, fearing he wouldn't sleep a wink all night. Gregor's snoring was louder than ever and Cassius's mind whirred with thoughts of his future. But his stomach was full of the tonic Sage had given him. It worked its magic as his body absorbed the powerful combination of ingredients.

Soon, he felt himself being pulled underneath the spell of a deep sleep and the dream that had evaded him since he'd arrived in The Bay of Laurel returned to him.

He was lying in a bed, just as he was in reality, but this mattress was woven from straw. His body felt so weak it was as if it belonged to someone else. Summoning all the energy he had, he lifted his hand and held it aloft, studying its familiar shape. Strong fingers. Smooth skin. Clean nails. There was no doubt this was the hand of a young man. A man perhaps not all that older than he was now. There were no lines. No wrinkles. No age spots or scars.

His other hand was being held and he felt the presence of someone he deeply loved. But the effort to turn his head and see who was there was too much.

His hand fell back beside him as if it weighed a ton and he moaned from the effort he'd expended. He was slipping away from this life.

That was as obvious to him as the rattled breathing that punctuated the silence in the room.

This is where Cassius's dream normally ended. He'd experienced it one hundred times and never gotten beyond this point. But he'd also never had one of Sage's sleeping tonics before. And if his conscious mind had been in any way in control, he'd have been surprised that this time, his dream continued.

Becoming aware of a sobbing, Cassius summoned all his strength and turned his head. Gabrielle was sitting beside him. She was holding his hand, her fingers threaded through his own.

"Cassius." A stream of tears ran down her beautiful face, leaving trails in the exquisite perfection of her delicate features.

He wanted to sit up. To take her in his arms, like he felt certain he'd done a thousand times before. To wrap his soul around hers in a dance of life and death.

But all he could do was blink up at her and draw in her essence.

"I love you," she whispered. "I know you need to let go. And that's okay. Because I'll see you again."

He could see the truth in her words. Feel the reality of them reverberating through his chest. He *would* see her again in whatever world lay waiting for them beyond this lifetime.

Then he was rising from the bed as his body turned to light. Beams of gold and blue and red sparked from the center of his being and poured into the room, cloaking Gabrielle, then letting her go as he rose higher and higher, until he was flying through the night sky.

His angel still had more she needed to do on this Earth, but his time was done.

Then Gregor was shaking him roughly by the shoulders and Cassius returned to his hut in The Bay of Laurel with a thud.

"Wake up!" Gregor shouted. "Wake up!"

Cassius moaned, trying to push Gregor away so he could return to the place where Gabrielle breathed the same air. Even if it meant he was dying. Because he knew without doubt he'd never change his path if it was one that took him away from his angel.

"You were crying," said Gregor. "Big sobbing sounds. You scared the life out of me."

"Sorry." Cassius let out a sigh. "Ironically, I was the one scaring the life out of myself."

"No wonder," Gregor huffed. "I'm surprised you didn't wake the entire kingdom. Now, go back to sleep and this time, try not to dream."

"Can't promise that." Cassius brought his right hand up to study it, just like he had in his dream. It was dark in the hut but he could still make out the shadows and lines. This was definitely the same hand.

Gregor returned to his own bed and pulled a blanket over himself.

Cassius brought his hand to his chest and placed it over his heart.

He now knew what he had to do. He'd stow away on the next carriage headed for Forte Cadence.

If it was inevitable that he was going to die young, he had no time to waste. They were meant to be together. Every day he lived without Gabrielle was a waste.

GABRIELLE

THE BEFORE

*G*abrielle woke with a stiff back and sharp headache. She'd slept on the stone floor of a large empty room where she'd been told to wait for the King.

Except, he never came.

The sun set and rose, and still the large doors to the room had yet to open. Gabrielle got up and stretched, her stomach growling and pressure building in her bladder. But there was no way she was going to leave this room. Not until she saw King Virtus.

Surely, he couldn't be too much longer?

She paced the room, watching the door, debating if she should try to get someone's attention. Was it possible that brute of a guard called Jaff had locked her in here with no intention of telling anyone she was? Now that she thought of it, this room was really very much like an oversized prison cell.

She went to the door and gripped the handle and was about to pull it open when it burst inward, toppling her over. She landed with a thud and looked up in horror to see the King leaning over her. Jaff and a different guard were standing either side of him.

The King put out his hand and relief slid through Gabrielle to think that maybe he had some redeemable features after all. But when she went to take his hand, he clenched it into a fist, with the exception of his index finger, and she realized he was pointing at her.

"What's the meaning of this?" he boomed, glaring at Gabrielle.

She clambered to her feet and smoothed down her dress, dropping to a curtsy with no idea if she was executing it correctly.

"Is this the girl?" The King turned to Jaff, who looked somewhat less cocky in his ruler's presence.

"Yes, Your Majesty." Jaff kept his gaze low, not looking King Virtus directly in the eye.

The King marched forward and two palace workers dressed in white scurried in behind him carrying a chair with a red velvet cushion. They placed the chair at the front of the room like a portable throne and scurried out. A third worker entered the room and placed a table beside the throne with a large bowl of fruit sitting on top.

King Virtus walked forward and sat down, the makeshift throne groaning as it took his weight. Gabrielle was relieved it didn't break. She needed the King in a good mood. She was already off to a bad enough start.

"Well?" he snapped, looking directly at Gabrielle as he picked up a bunch of purple grapes. "What is it that's so important you're holding up our breakfast? We've been told you have an important message for us."

Gabrielle glanced at Jaff, then back at the King.

"May we speak in private?" she asked.

"That's preposterous!" The King tipped back his head and laughed. "Nobody speaks to us alone."

"Just you," said Gabrielle. "I wish to speak to you alone."

The King shovelled a handful of grapes into his mouth and chewed loudly as his cheeks bulged. "And we already told you that we don't speak to anybody alone."

"Oh." She bowed her head, realizing he was speaking about himself in plural form. His girth was certainly wide enough to warrant being considered two people.

"Well, get on with it, girl," King Virtus snapped, spitting out a stem from one of the grapes at her feet.

Gabrielle held out her hands. "I come to you armed with information, not weapons. I have your best interests at heart. Please, Your Majesty, may I speak with you alone?"

"Get. On. With. It." The King glared at her. "Or would you prefer to spend some time in our dungeon to consider how you came here to waste your King's time?"

"It's about The Bay of Laurel," said Gabrielle, seeing no choice but to speak to him with an audience present. "Their Guardians are coming to the market and taking people."

The King belched loudly and rolled his eyes. "Not this again. We've already been told. We're very well aware."

"You're not worried about it?" Gabrielle asked, aware she was about to be thrown out at any moment.

"A lion cannot build an army made of rats." The King scratched at his beard.

"But what if the rats were fed and nurtured and they grew into lions?" Gabrielle asked. "What if they were given magical tonics and became strong and fearsome?"

The King seemed to find this amusing. He picked up a long slice of melon, pointed it at Gabrielle and shook his head before eating it in two bites.

"The people are happy in The Bay of Laurel," Gabrielle said. "They're well fed and trained to fight. As soon as word gets out, people will be lining up to go next. They'll walk to the border if they have to. You'll be left to rule over a kingdom that's built from nothing more than flies and dust."

This wiped the smile from the King's face and he stood from his throne, glaring at Gabrielle.

"How would you know this?" he boomed. "How could you possibly know any of this? Have you been to this other kingdom?"

"No, Your Majesty." Gabrielle shrank back, both from his anger and his rancid breath.

"Have you spoken to someone who's been there?" he asked.

"No, Your Majesty."

King Virtus looked up at Jaff. "Take her to the dungeon. Give her two days to think about herself. Then clean her up and bring her back to me. I'm in the market for a new wench."

Gabrielle flinched. Coming here was a mistake. Why had she thought the King would listen to her? It's clear he doesn't listen to anyone, let alone a girl from the Valley.

Jaff gripped her by the arm and led her from the room. The other guard marched alongside and she was grateful he didn't touch her. Jaff was inflicting enough pain all on his own.

"I've got this," said Jaff, dragging her through the corridors.

The second guard shrugged and turned away. Jaff really didn't seem to have a lot of respect amongst his colleagues.

"I can walk," she protested. "You're hurting my arm."

"It's more fun like that." Jaff sneered and Gabrielle felt even more sorry for his pretty wife back home. It was no wonder she was seeking comfort in another man's arms.

They reached the top of a staircase that headed straight down and Jaff paused.

"I gave you a choice last night, and you made a poor decision," he whispered roughly in her ear. "You chose the King over me. So, now I'm going to give you another choice."

Gabrielle swallowed, nodding her head slightly to show she heard him.

"I can take you to the dungeon," he said. "Where you'll be hungry. And cold. And filthy."

"What's the other choice?" Gabrielle asked, deciding just about anything had to be better than that. Except the one thing he was most likely to suggest.

"Or I lock you in the hen house," he sneered. "There's food and water in there and I can return later when I'm off duty and we can continue that inspection I gave you earlier. What do you say?"

"The hen house." Surely, it had to be easier to escape from there than a stone cell in the King's dungeon?

Jaff licked his lips. "Smart choice."

He took her further down the corridor and after a couple of turns they reached a thick wooden door. He threw it open and took Gabrielle outside, leading her into the garden.

"If you try to escape, I won't be as merciful as the King." He pulled her around a bend in the path to a wooden shed.

"What did he do to the Queen?" Gabrielle asked, remembering the King's final comment to her. "Is she okay?"

"How would I know?" Jaff threw open the door and pushed Gabrielle inside. Several chickens darted out of her way, clucking with annoyance.

She turned around to see the door slam and heard a bolt slide through the lock.

"If you escape, I will find you," Jaff said through the door. "And bad luck or good luck, I'll kill you with the knife you seemed to know so much about."

"King Virtus asked to see me again in two days," she called through the door. "Won't he wonder what happened to me when I go missing?"

Jaff scoffed. "Unlikely. Do you know how many girls like you he has locked up in his dungeon? And if you're as special as you seem to think you are, and he does notice, we'll tell him you curled up and died. Not unusual in that place."

Gabrielle's eyes flared. How many deaths was the King responsible for? It did seem like something awful had happened to his wife. Then again, the queens in this kingdom were never known to live long or happy lives.

"I'll be back faster than you expect," said Jaff. "Although, you probably already knew that being able to see the future and all."

She clenched her fists as the sound of his laughter faded down the path. A chicken flew at her leg and she jumped back, letting out a gasp.

The chicken scuttled away, and she looked around her unusual prison. The sturdy walls were lined with nesting boxes and the floor was covered in coarse sand. There was a small hole up high in one of the walls where the chickens came in and out from their yard, but she'd be lucky to be able to get her head through there let alone her whole body.

This visit hadn't gone as well as she'd hoped, but she'd also had quite a bit of good fortune. The liking that Jaff had taken to her would hopefully be what saved her. There had to be a way out of this hen house. Or maybe one of the palace staff would come in to feed the chickens and she could escape while they weren't looking.

She began checking the walls, looking for a weak panel or way she could break out. But it seemed everything had been nailed tight. Had Jaff used this as his own personal cell before? It seemed more secure than any other hen house she'd seen before.

She kicked at one of the walls, admitting she hadn't seen many other hen houses. Keeping animals was a luxury in the Valley of the Blessed that very few could afford. It was hard enough for the people to keep themselves alive, let alone have another mouth to feed. This reminded her of the woman with the goat who'd come to see her, refusing to believe that her son's illness was being caused by the milk. Hopefully the boy was still alive and hadn't died from his mother's refusal to take good advice.

There was a noise at the door and Gabrielle scurried behind one of the nesting boxes and crouched down. It would be better to escape unseen. After a night without food or water, she didn't have the energy to outrun anyone on a race down the mountain. And she was unlikely to escape the dungeon a second time.

Gabrielle steadied her breathing and tried to make herself small while she waited for the door to open.

CASSIUS

THE BEFORE

Cassius walked to the tavern the next morning alongside Gregor. Despite the vividness of his dreams, he'd slept well after the tonic Sage had made him.

"That was some nightmare you had," Gregor commented.

"It actually wasn't so bad." He smiled. "I mean, I'm not so sure about the way it ended, but I got to see someone I care about so that was nice."

He thought about the tender way Gabrielle had held his hand and the tears she'd wept. The sort that were reserved only for someone you really loved.

"You got a girl back home?" Gregor asked.

"No," he said. "Or maybe yes."

Gregor chuckled. "Oh, one of those situations."

"Yeah, something like that." Cassius knew he had no hope of trying to explain. He didn't even understand it himself. "How are you feeling today?"

"Guilty." Gregor smiled sadly. "Life here is good. My mind's clear. My body's strong. All I want is for my son to feel the same. He's been so sick. I don't even know if he's still alive."

"I'm sorry to hear that." Cassius patted him on the back and was struck with a vision of a goat.

"What's the matter?" Gregor asked, noticing the odd expression on his face.

"Nothing," said Cassius, well used to covering up his gift. His family had never understood it. It's unlikely Gregor would either.

"It can't be nothing," Gregor pressed. "You look like you've seen a ghost."

Cassius laughed. "For some reason I was thinking about goats, not ghosts. Do goats mean anything to you?"

Gregor stopped walking and gave him a strange look. "Not you, too."

Cassius pressed his palm to his chest. "What do you mean?"

"My wife went to see a fortune teller, not long before I was taken by the Guardians," Gregor said. "She was completely fake. Told my wife that it was our goat making our son sick, which is ridiculous. That animal's milk was the only thing keeping our boy alive."

Cassius took this in. Gregor must be talking about Gabrielle who was anything but fake. And Cassius himself had seen a goat when he'd touched Gregor as he spoke of his son being unwell.

"Come on." He walked on, deciding not to say anything more. He had to share a hut with this guy and he was clearly not a believer. "I must be hungry and dreaming of goat stew."

Gregor pulled a face. "It would taste better than those tonics."

They reached the tavern and went inside, heading for the table lined with cups. Cassius purposefully lost Gregor in the crowd and wove his way behind the table to a door at the back of the tavern. Knocking gently, he opened the door and stepped through, finding himself in the room he'd sat in last night while Sage had made his sleeping tonic.

There was a small girl with dark hair sitting at the table, stripping leaves from an enormous pile of rosemary stalks.

"Mom!" she shouted. "There's a man."

Sage rushed from the back room with a look of alarm on her face that instantly softened when she saw Cassius.

"It's okay, Ariel," she soothed. "This man won't hurt you."

"Because he's an angel?" Ariel asked, her wise eyes seeming decades too old for her small body.

"That's right." Sage turned to Cassius. "How did you sleep?"

"Better than ever," he said. "And worse than ever."

"You had dreams?" she asked, pushing out a chair and motioning for him to sit down.

"I dreamed of my angel." He sank into his chair and accepted the tonic Sage set down in front of him. "Only this time the dream went further. I saw her face."

"And it was the angel you've met." Sage said this more as a statement than a question. "Cassius, you should also know that you don't need to see someone's face to be able to recognize them."

Cassius nodded. This was true. The moment Gabrielle had first held his hands, he'd known she was his angel.

"I'm going to go back to her," he said, taking a long sip of his tonic. This one was even more bitter than their daily tonics. Quite the opposite to the one he'd been given last night. "My dream convinced me of that. I'll hide in one of the empty carriages."

"That's not allowed," said little Ariel, setting down a rosemary stalk. "It's against the rules."

He winked at this serious girl. "Well, I'd better not get caught then."

Her eyes widened and she grinned. "You will get caught. But you'll be okay."

Cassius turned to Sage, his jaw dropping. "Does your daughter know this or is she guessing?"

Sage smiled warmly. "I'm not sure just yet. She's still young."

"The Guardians were loading their carriage this morning," said Ariel. "I saw them."

"I have to go." Cassius stood. "This could be my best chance."

"Drink your tonic," said Sage. "It's a special blend that will sustain you for several days if needed."

Cassius drained his cup, then narrowed his brows at Sage. "How did you know I'd need it?"

She laughed. "Are you really asking me that?"

Pulling back his shoulders, Cassius felt more certain than ever that the decision he'd made was the right one. If Sage had already known he was going to make it, then surely it was the path he was meant to take. Even Ariel had said he'd be okay, despite also being adamant he was going to get caught. Hopefully she was wrong about that bit.

"Thank you," he said, knowing he didn't need to elaborate. Sage knew exactly what impact she'd had on his life.

She brought her hand to her heart. "You only have yourself to thank."

Cassius headed for the door.

"You could go to Wintergreen," said Ariel, just as he touched the handle. "It's the kingdom of flowers. They have a magician who makes potions."

"Elixirs," Sage corrected. "And it's an alchemist, not a magician."

"I don't know a lot about the other kingdoms, I'm afraid," said Cassius. Traveling between the world's five kingdoms was considered highly dangerous. For the vast majority of the population, the kingdom you were born in was the one where you remained.

"This is the kingdom of taste," said Sage. "Our power comes from the food we eat. Wintergreen is the kingdom of scent. They make powerful smelling elixirs from the oils of their plants. The Sands of Naar controls their people by touch, or rather forbidding their people from using this sense. Feldspar mines for crystals to harness the power of sight."

"And what about Forte Cadence?" asked Cassius. "The only sense you've left out is hearing. And there's nothing to be heard back home, except the sound of our King digesting his food."

"Your kingdom is yet to discover its power," said Sage. "When it does, it will have the chance to be the most powerful kingdom of all."

Cassius thought about this for a moment. "You said last night that my angel was going to change the world."

Sage nodded. "I did."

"Will she discover the power for Forte Cadence?" he asked.

"That's a question for your angel," said Sage. "Oh, and if you're going to the carriages, you'd be better off to leave by the other door."

Cassius nodded, shot Ariel a friendly smile, then rushed to the door he'd entered through last night.

"Wait!" Sage went to him and for a moment he thought she was going to embrace him. But instead, she put something into the pocket of his shirt. "It's only bread. But it has a few extra ingredients to help you on your way."

He put his hand on Sage's arm, unsure how he'd ever be able to thank her for her kindness. Although, she wasn't the sort who wanted gratitude. She made her decisions based on what she thought was right. And for whatever reason, she'd decided Cassius was not only an angel, but one who needed her help.

He emerged into the herb garden and darted around the various plants to the other side, peering around a lavender bush as he watched the Guardians loading a carriage, readying it for its next trip to Forte Cadence.

He'd worked out there were two carriages used for this purpose. The other had left the day before. It wasn't going to be easy to sneak on board, but if he could manage it, he should be able to hide amongst the pile of blankets stowed in the back.

Except, one of the Guardians was keeping watch over the doors, while another tended to the mules. It seemed they were taking no chances.

A flash of movement darted past, and Ariel appeared in front of the Guardian at the rear of the carriage. She held out a bowl, her tiny frame towered over by the giant Guardian.

"That smells good," the Guardian said, smiling broadly.

"It's for your journey," said Ariel. "The herbalist made it."

The Guardian reached out an enormous hand and Ariel darted away.

"First, you have to catch me!" she giggled.

The Guardian roared. Not with anger but amusement as he took a series of large strides after Ariel.

Cassius knew exactly why Ariel was enticing the Guardian into this game, and he didn't miss his chance. He ran forward and slipped into the carriage, burying himself under the pile of blankets and trying to still his breath.

"Got you!" the Guardian shouted, his deep laugh practically shaking the carriage.

Cassius froze, thinking for one moment the Guardian was talking to him. Then he realized it was nothing more than the game of tag and he was talking to Ariel.

"No fair," Ariel complained. "You're bigger than me."

"And hungrier," he said. "Hand over the bread or I might decide to have little girl for my supper."

Ariel laughed, seeming to feel secure in this giant's presence. Cassius smiled in the darkness, grateful to this new friend he'd made and would likely never see again.

Several minutes later the carriage doors slammed closed and there was a lurch of movement.

He'd made his decision and it was too late to back out now.

He was on his way home to Forte Cadence. Back to his angel. And to what he was sure would be his inevitable death.

GABRIELLE

THE BEFORE

Gabrielle's eyes widened in the darkness. It wasn't a palace worker who'd entered the hen house, but a small boy. She stared at him for several long seconds before realizing who she was looking at.

Prince Virtus. Heir to the throne and future King of Forte Cadence. Which meant that one day he'd be the most powerful man in the world.

The Prince closed the door behind him and strutted into the hen house like a cockerel.

"Hey, little hennies," he clucked. The hens scattered in response, seeming even less keen to greet the Prince than they had been to see Gabrielle.

The boy squatted down, his healthy belly protruding over the waistband of his finely tailored trousers.

"Come now, little hennies." He held out his hand with what looked like seed piled up on his palm.

One hen ventured forward cautiously, keen to inspect what the prince had for them. It pecked at his hand, seeming pleased with the offering.

"Ouch!" Prince Virtus stood and shook the remaining seeds onto the ground. "That hurt!"

He kicked out, the tip of his pointed leather boot sending the hen squawking and fluttering to the other side of the enclosure.

"I am the Prince," the boy said, clutching his hand to his chest. "Actually, no. *We* are the Prince."

Gabrielle wondered if maybe she should show herself. If she could somehow befriend this child, perhaps she could have some influence in the future over the future of the kingdom.

Then she caught sight of her tattered dress and filthy feet and knew she was the last person the Prince would want to befriend. He'd see her as nothing more than a peasant girl, like his father had.

The boy stalked toward the hens who scattered and clucked loudly in response. "Which one of you was it? Which one of you dared to hurt us?"

The hens moved further away, some making their escape to the yard, while others jostled to push through the small hole in the wall. It seemed these creatures were familiar with the Prince. And not one of them wanted to find out what he had to say.

"It was you!" Prince Virtus grabbed a chicken roughly by the neck and lifted it off the ground. "You did it. You hurt my—our—hand."

The Prince took the terrified hen to one of the nesting beds. Feathers flew and the poor animal squawked as this awful child held the hen down and choked it until it lay still.

He pulled back, wiping some sweat from his forehead with his sleeve and giving the creature a satisfied smile.

Gabrielle put her hand over her mouth to stop herself from sobbing. This wasn't a child she could befriend. This child was…a monster.

"You were only a girl, anyway," the Prince said to hen. "Like Mother was."

Was? Gabrielle felt certain the Queen must be dead. And she feared it had happened in the same way the Prince had re-enacted. What hope did he have of growing up to be a decent leader when he had his evil father as a role model?

The poor Queen. Poor everyone, really. Including this awful boy who may not have been quite so awful had he been born to different parents.

What hope did any of them have?

"Prince Virtus!" a female voice called. "Are you in there?"

A woman wearing an apron entered the barn and marched over to him. She looked familiar, although it was too hard to tell for sure in the dim light if Gabrielle had met her before. Perhaps she'd done a reading for her one time.

"I've been looking for you everywhere!" the woman said, and Gabrielle decided she must be the Prince's nursemaid. Which meant it was highly unlikely they'd ever met.

"We were teaching lessons." The Prince pulled back his shoulders.

The nursemaid glanced over to the nesting bed and let out an audible groan. "What have you done?"

"She pecked us," said the Prince, holding out his hand. "She deserved what she got. Just like—"

"That's enough, Your Highness," the nursemaid said, her voice trembling. "You weren't even meant to be in here. It's off limits for repair today. It could have been dangerous."

So, that's what Jaff must have told them.

"Nothing is off limits to us," the boy said. "This hen house belongs to me. Everything in this kingdom belongs to me. Including you."

He stared at his nursemaid in a way that sent a shiver down Gabrielle's spine. This boy couldn't be more than five years old, and already he'd learned to speak to people in this way.

Seeming to be used to being treated like this, the nursemaid pointed to the door. "Run along while I clean up this mess."

"No." The Prince scowled at her, jamming his hands on his hips. "We want to pull out the feathers."

"Your Highness," the nursemaid said, doing her best to sound stern yet affectionate. "That is not how a Prince behaves. Do you see your father pulling feathers out of hens?"

The boy locked his eyes on the nursemaid. "No, but I saw him put his hands around Mother's neck."

Gabrielle gasped and the nursemaid's eyes darted over to the dark corner where she was hiding. Thankfully, the boy hadn't seemed to hear.

"Then take the hen outside with you," the nursemaid said. "It could be dangerous in here until the repairs are finished."

"Then why are you staying?" the Prince asked cautiously. He may be evil, but it seemed this boy was no fool.

"I'll be out in a moment," the nursemaid said, ushering the boy and his prize to the door. Thankfully, the Prince did as he was told, which seemed to be an unusual occurrence.

As the door opened, the light poured in, and Gabrielle saw the nursemaid had the most beautiful red hair. She held back a second gasp when she realized why the woman was familiar. She was the same one Gabrielle had seen in her vision of Jaff's wife.

"I won't hurt you," the nursemaid said, closing the door and turning to face the dark corner Gabrielle had hoped would hide her. "You can come out now."

Gabrielle stepped cautiously from the shadows and cast her eyes down, aware she was completely at the mercy of this woman.

"Please," she said. "Please let me go."

The nursemaid held up a hand. "If I let you go, will I ever see you around here again?"

Gabrielle shook her head. "I came here to speak to the King. He made it very clear that he isn't interested in anything I have to say."

"I could have told you that and saved you the trouble." The nursemaid pulled an apple from her apron pocket and held it out. "Here, have this."

"Thank you." Gabrielle took it gratefully and bit into the sweet flesh, closing her eyes at the sheer pleasure of it.

"You're the one who sees the future, aren't you?" The nursemaid tilted her head. "My name's Amba. My husband told me about you last night. He's the guard who took you to the King."

Gabrielle chewed slowly and nodded, deciding to trust this woman.

"What do you see for me?" Amba asked, putting out her hand. "What's my future?"

"It doesn't work like that," Gabrielle lied, not wanting to see what lay ahead for this woman who was married to the most despicable of men.

"I need to know." Amba's eyes filled with tears. "You're already aware of what my husband's like. Is there any hope for me?"

Gabrielle took her hand and was filled with a sense of profound misery and darkness.

"What is it?" Amba asked. "What do you see?"

"Come with me," Gabrielle said, hoping that was an answer enough. "I'm going to The Bay of Laurel."

"But the Guardians have been abducting people." Amba appeared horrified. "I've heard the screams when I've been in the market. Why would you want to go there?"

"There's food," said Gabrielle. "The people are happy. *You* could be happy."

She seemed genuinely torn. "But, I…"

"Here you have nothing," said Gabrielle. "There you have a potential future. Far from where your husband will ever be able to find you."

"It was him that put you in here, wasn't it?" Amba asked. She must already have known this for fact, but clearly needed to hear it.

"Yes." Gabrielle nodded. "But he hadn't yet put a finger on me if that makes you feel better. Unless you count the way he dragged me here."

"I'll come," said Amba quietly. "Because if my husband doesn't kill me, I know the Prince will one day."

Gabrielle swallowed, unable to deny she was likely very right.

Maybe this is what her gift was really about. If she could learn to shape the future, maybe she could make this kingdom a better place.

CASSIUS

THE BEFORE

*T*he carriage rolled along the road slowly. Cassius wasn't sure why, and he wasn't in a position to find out. Eventually, they picked up speed and headed in what he assumed was the direction of Forte Cadence. Or more to the point, in the direction of Gabrielle.

From listening to the voices, he was fairly certain there were four Guardians riding at the front of the carriage.

He climbed out from underneath the blankets and stretched out his body. It felt good to move again and his muscles ached before they adjusted to the freedom of movement.

The carriage was far more comfortable without being crowded with other people. Far more pleasant too without the sound of sobbing or the stench of so many bodies crowded into such a small space. He wondered if the woman who'd cried so much on the journey over was still upset about the change in direction her life had taken. Gregor didn't seem to be. Aside from missing his son, of course.

Cassius intended to check on the boy once he returned to Forte Cadence. Assuming he could find the house. Not too many homes had a goat, so that would narrow it down. But how might he stop the boy from drinking the goat's milk? He could steal the goat...although, that didn't seem fair. The rest of the family was dependent on the milk. Which also ruled out poisoning the animal—aside from the fact that would be cruel. The goat never asked for her milk to be taken. He'd just have to try talking to Gregor's wife and hope that she listened to him. Perhaps he could convince her to take her son on the next carriage and find her way to The Bay of Laurel? That would cure her son. He hadn't seen one single goat there.

The thought of drinking milk prompted his stomach to give him the first signs of feeling hungry. Thankfully, the tonic Sage had made for him had tied him over well, as she said it would. He had the piece of bread tucked in his pocket, but decided to save it for when he was properly hungry.

Cassius paced the carriage, keeping his footsteps light, but when it left the smooth earth of The Bay of Laurel and headed onto the bumpy roads that would lead to Forte Cadence, he was forced to sit back down. If he were thrown against one of the walls, it might alert the Guardians to his presence. He'd already decided if that happened, he'd do his very best to slip out of their grasp and run. They might be taller than him. And stronger. But Cassius had always been fast. The only reason they'd caught him back at the market was because he was making sure they didn't take Gabrielle.

Cassius buried his head in his hands, knowing this protective streak may have had very damaging consequences for Gabrielle. If only he'd known how well the people in The Bay of Laurel lived, he'd have let them take her. Perhaps he'd have ended up there himself and that's where the scene from his dream would take place. Maybe it still will?

Because as much as Sage had said he'd be unable to escape his premature death, she had also said there were aspects of his life that he could control. And maybe the quality of the life he led with Gabrielle was one of them. In any case, he wanted to make sure she had the best possible life for as long as he was able.

The carriage trundled along the road until the light that peeked through the gaps in the timber began to fade. Soon, he'd be back in Forte Cadence and with the angel from his dreams.

GABRIELLE

THE BEFORE

*G*abrielle and Amba snuck out of the hen house, leaving the door ajar so that the creatures had at least some chance of escaping Prince Virtus. Like them.

Except it wasn't just the Prince they were escaping. It was Jaff and his leering eyes and roaming hands.

With their hearts beating wildly, they tiptoed past Prince Virtus. Although, they need not have bothered given how engrossed he was in de-feathering his kill. Amba led the way, taking Gabrielle through the forest that ringed the castle and onto the rocky path that went down Mount Allegro. They kept quiet for fear of being discovered, neither of them daring to speak a word. Twice, Gabrielle stumbled on a loose rock and had to clamp her hand over her mouth to stop herself from gasping.

Soon they'd be in the Valley of the Blessed and could make their way to The Bay of Laurel.

To Cassius.

Gabrielle was running toward love, yet it occurred to her that Amba was running away from it. Because part of her must have loved Jaff at one stage in her life, surely? Unless she'd had as little say in that union as Gabrielle would have if she'd been stuck inside the hen house awaiting his return.

They broke through the trees and into the sunlight and Gabrielle was overcome with a feeling of intense happiness. She may not have achieved what she came here for, but she'd managed to get away unharmed. And she'd hopefully been able to save Amba's life.

The paused, doubling over and gasping for breath, reveling in the feeling of safety now that they'd put some distance between themselves and the castle.

Amba began to giggle.

"What's funny?" Gabrielle asked, as they picked their way over the rocks.

"I can't believe I'm actually doing this." Amba shook her head. "I've never done anything so crazy in my life."

"It's not crazy," said Gabrielle. "It's brave."

They lapsed back into thoughtful silence as Gabrielle waited for her eyes to adjust to the bright light. The terrain on the lower part of Mount Allegro was bare, without a tree or shrub in sight. But what it lacked in flora, it made up for in rocks. And them some more rocks. This was where years ago Gabrielle had found the rock she used in her tent as her crystal ball.

"Queen Starla was brave," Amba whispered. "Brave doesn't always work out so well."

"The King killed her, didn't he?" Gabrielle asked. "The Prince said he put his hands around her neck."

Amba let out an anguished sob. "He choked her to death at the breakfast table right in front of my eyes. It's such a relief to be able to say that out loud."

"You didn't tell anyone?" Gabrielle wrapped an arm around her new friend. "Not even your husband?"

"Wouldn't want to give him ideas." Amba huffed. "Plus it would be an act of heresy to speak out against the King. I knew if I told anybody, I'd be next."

"You're doing the right thing by leaving," said Gabrielle.

"What did you really see in the vision you told Jaff about?" Amba stared ahead, reluctant to make eye contact.

"What did he tell you I saw?" Gabrielle ventured, letting go of Amba so she could concentrate on not tripping over as she walked.

"He said that you saw me whoring myself around and that he would be forced to kill my lover to save me from disgrace." Amba's voice broke with emotion. "He said you told him he shouldn't kill the man, but he didn't care and that he was looking forward to the day so he could kill us both."

"Right." Gabrielle turned this alternative version of events around in her head.

"I'm not a whore!" Amba cried. "I don't have a lover."

Gabrielle put a gentle hand on her back. "I believe you. And that's not what I told Jaff. Well, not exactly. To be honest, I wouldn't blame you if you did seek comfort in another man's arms. A man who actually has a heart."

"But none of that matters now, right?" said Amba. "Because I'm free of him. He can't kill me when I'm in another kingdom."

"That's right." Gabrielle smiled. "Your new life is beginning today."

Amba looped her hand in the crook of Gabrielle's arm. "I'm so glad I met you. Jaff thought he was saving you for himself, but little did he know, he was saving you for me."

Gabrielle patted Amba's hand. They made their way down the mountain, the afternoon light starting to fade by the time they reached the bottom.

"How often do the Guardians come?" Amba asked.

"There's no warning," said Gabrielle. "We can wait in my tent for them. It could be days. It could be weeks. But we'll hear them when they arrive."

Amba seemed concerned by this. "What if Jaff comes looking for me?"

"I have a good hiding place in the back of my tent." She hoped it would be good enough if they needed it. "I'll keep you sa—"

Her words were cut off by a terrible scream floating up from the village.

"Is that them?" Amba asked, stepping up her pace. "Could we be that lucky?"

Gabrielle sighed. "I think we're due for some good luck. Although, I may have used up my share when you let me out of the hen house."

"That wasn't luck," she said. "I knew you'd be in there. I just hadn't realized the Prince had plans to sneak in there too."

They reached the village and Gabrielle took Amba's hand and led her through the market. People were running and screaming and they fought to walk toward the square, like a fish trying to swim against the tide.

"Guardians!" several people shouted at them, not understanding why they weren't running in fear. "Get away!"

"Hurry!" Gabrielle pulled a startled Amba down the alley faster. It could be days until they came back again.

They got to the market square where there was indeed a Guardian's carriage being loaded with people. The rest of the square was empty and Gabrielle rushed over to the carriage.

Amba let out a whimper as she caught sight of the huge Guardians. One of them turned as they approached, seeming startled. Nobody had come toward them willingly before.

"What do you want?" he growled. "We've made our choices. Be off with you."

"Take us," Gabrielle pleaded. "Please, we'd like to be of service to your kingdom. I'm stronger than I look. And my friend here is a crack shot with a bow and arrow."

Amba gripped her hand, clearly not in possession of any such skill. But their talents were unlikely to be tested here. The carriages normally left much earlier than this. The Guardians would be keen to get away to put some distance behind them before nightfall.

"The carriage is full." The Guardian put up his hand.

"Surely, there's room for two more." Gabrielle smiled sweetly. "Please, sir."

A second Guardian approached, and it took two beats for Gabrielle to realize she was female. With short hair and broad shoulders, she looked every bit as strong as her male counterparts.

"Why do you want to come?" the woman asked. "Nobody ever wants to come with us."

"We're not like everybody," Gabrielle said, smiling warmly.

The Guardian put her hand on Gabrielle's arm and she knew instantly that this woman was good.

"We'd like to make a fresh start," said Gabrielle, lowering her voice. "My friend here needs to get away. Quite urgently."

Amba was trembling beside her, looking at the ground as she waited for her fate to be decided.

"We can't," the Guardian said. "I'm sorry."

"It's a matter of life or death," Gabrielle whispered. "Please."

The Guardian seemed torn, glancing from the carriage, which looked far from full, and back to the two skinny girls begging for her help.

"Load 'em on," she instructed.

The male Guardian didn't seem at all pleased to be overruled but did as he was directed and held the door open for Gabrielle and Amba.

They climbed into the darkness, their future life awaiting with just as much mystery.

"It's you," a male voice gasped.

Gabrielle's heart surged, thinking for one crazy moment it might be Cassius, even though that made no sense.

As her eyes adjusted, she saw it was the man she'd given a reading to in her tent. The one she'd told would have a happier life in The Bay of Laurel than in Forte Cadence.

But now that she looked at him, she realized where else she'd seen him—in her vision of Jaff. The man cowering at his feet was this same man. When she'd seen Jaff's pretty wife and her lover in her vision, she hadn't realized that soon, she would know them both.

"I took your advice," the man said. "And if you're coming with us, then I now know you weren't lying to me."

"I only told you what I saw," said Gabrielle as she and Amba sat down beside him. "That's all I ever do."

"My name's Lark," he said, doing his best to make room.

"I'm Gabrielle." She smiled at him. "And this is Amba."

Amba dipped her gaze, seeming shy, while Lark's gaze was drawn to her.

It's warmed Gabrielle's heart, making everything she'd just been through seem worthwhile. These two were always meant to meet. And Gabrielle was the one who was supposed to bring them together.

Perhaps her gift wasn't a curse if it could bring about beauty like this. Amba had been destined for a life of misery in the castle and now she had a whole future stretching out before her. With Lark.

Now all Gabrielle had to do was hope that changing their paths meant a new future could come true.

For all of them.

Because she wasn't ready to find Cassius, then lose him all over again.

CASSIUS

THE BEFORE

Cassius must have drifted off to sleep. He woke to the sound of another carriage passing them on the road.

He sat up with his heart racing, unsure why he was feeling this way. All his senses were screaming at him to pay attention. It was like the pull he'd felt that night when he'd found himself walking to Sage's garden. The universe was trying desperately to tell him something, but he couldn't correctly read the signs.

Pressing his hands to the side of the carriage, Cassius closed his eyes and tried to understand why he was feeling like this. An image of Gabrielle entered his mind, which was even more confusing. Although, not unusual given he thought of her most of the time.

He could see her reaching out to him, her eyes filled with anguish and a wave a realization passed over him. She was in the other carriage! He was certain of it. While he was making his way to Forte Cadence to find her, she was headed to The Bay of Laurel to do the same for him.

He groaned, resting his forehead against the carriage and balling his hands into fists. This was a disaster. They were both so determined to see each other that their actions had cancelled each other's out. Now they were still going to end up being kingdoms apart, it's just that they were swapping kingdoms.

At least Gabrielle would finally get something decent to eat. And maybe he could find his way back to The Bay of Laurel somehow. Although, something told him he wasn't going to be welcome given he'd gone to such lengths to get away.

"Gabrielle," he whispered to the night air as the two carriages headed away from each other.

The mules pulled the carriage to a stop and Cassius's heart beat hard with both excitement and fear as he prepared to hide under the blankets. He'd forgotten the mules needed to be rested overnight to ensure they had enough food and water. Maybe when the Guardians fell asleep, he could sneak out and see if Gabrielle's carriage had also stopped.

Listening hard, he was certain he could no longer hear the other carriage moving along the road. Then he remembered he was locked in and the Guardians had no reason to open the doors.

Gabrielle was *right there.* And he had no way of getting to her. He had to find a way out.

Feeling along the timber planks that made up the carriage, he desperately searched for a weakness. But this prison on wheels was sealed tight.

He slumped against the doors, no longer caring if the Guardians opened them and found him. What was the worst that could happen? They would return him to The Bay of Laurel? Now that he knew that's where Gabrielle was headed, that sounded like a fine idea. Although, would they let him live in the village alongside them? More likely, they'd take him to Forte Cadence and leave him there to starve. They could only save so many people, which meant there was little point in saving someone who didn't want to be saved.

Muffled voices floated across the night air as the other carriage released its cargo, allowing them a few moments of fresh air before they'd be bundled up inside for the night.

"Gabrielle," Cassius whispered, knowing it was impossible for her to hear him.

A shriek rang out in the distance, followed by the sound of boots pounding the earth. Something was going on. Cassius got to his feet wondering if Gabrielle had made a run for it. That seemed unlikely given she was on her way to find him. Perhaps someone else had seen their chance to get away and decided to take it?

He pressed his ear to the carriage doors, trying to hear what was happening outside. The sounds were getting further away the more he listened, so he held his breath.

A soft clunk had him leaping back as he realized it was the plank of wood used to secure the door being lifted. Glancing at the blankets, he decided not to hide himself. This was his chance to use the element of surprise to leap from the shadows and out into the night.

He pressed himself to the wall of the carriage and waited as one of the doors creaked open. As soon as the Guardian stepped inside, he needed to take his chance.

"Cassius," a soft voice called. "It's me."

With eyes wide open, he stepped into the sliver of moonlight and saw Gabrielle peering into the carriage.

"My angel," he breathed. "How did you know I was here?"

"I don't know." She smiled as he jumped down to the ground. "Quickly, while the Guardians are distracted."

He took her hand, and warmth spread up his arm, directly to his heart.

Together, they ran into the shadows, not sure where they were heading, but happy as long as they were by each other's side.

GABRIELLE

THE BEFORE

Gabrielle ran silently beside Cassius, hardly able to believe her instincts had been so accurate. As soon as the carriage had left Forte Cadence, she'd felt herself drawing nearer to him. When they'd stopped for the mules to rest, the feeling had intensified to the point she could no longer concentrate on anything else.

It wasn't until Amba had pointed out she'd heard another carriage that she'd realized what had her feeling like that.

Somehow, Cassius was in the other carriage. Which was crazy given nobody was ever returned to Forte Cadence after the Guardians had taken them. Then again, nobody was like Cassius. He was coming back to her. She knew it with the same force as one of her clearest visions.

As soon as they'd been let out of the carriage, she'd taken Amba by the hand and explained in hurried whispers what she needed to do. More to the point, what she needed Amba to do.

Make a distraction so Gabrielle could see if she was right, rather than spend the rest of her life wondering.

Amba's eyes had filled with tears at the thought of having to continue alone, but she'd nodded, grateful for the life Gabrielle had saved her from.

After that, things had taken off quickly. Lark had overheard Gabrielle's request and before Amba could step one foot away from the Guardians, he'd run as fast as he could before pretending to trip over a tree root and sprain his ankle. He'd shrieked and howled and been so convincing that Gabrielle had taken a few seconds to launch herself into motion.

As the guards had run over to Lark, Gabrielle had gone to the other carriage and opened the door. If she was wrong, she planned to claim she was confused and thought that was the carriage she'd arrived in.

But she hadn't been wrong.

She'd opened the door and there he'd been.

Cassius.

Her Cassius, as she'd come to think of him, even though she had no claim over him at all.

"Stop," she eventually panted as their running became too much. "I need to catch my breath."

Cassius pulled her behind a tree and she let go of his hand, doubling over to steady her breathing. A dizzy feeling wrapped itself around her head like a swarm of wasps.

Cassius held something out to her, but she couldn't make it out in the darkness.

"It's bread," he whispered. "Eat it."

"It's yours," she protested. "I can't."

"I've had plenty," he said. "Trust me. More food than I've eaten in my life. You should see The Bay of Laurel."

"I've seen it in my dreams." She took a bite of the bread, closing her eyes at the sustenance.

"Sometimes, things are even more beautiful in real life than they are in dreams." He reached out and ran his fingertips down her arm, making it obvious he was no longer talking about the kingdom.

Gabrielle swallowed the bread and smiled. "Did you come back for me?"

"Yes." He edged a little closer. "Did you go looking for me?"

"Yes." She found his lips in the night, not needing the light of any stars to guide her. This is the person she'd been searching for all her life, even though she'd never known it. She'd spent so much time alone, trying to survive. Now she knew why it was all worth it.

Because Cassius was worth it.

He kissed her, the warmth of his soft lips pressing tenderly against hers at first, then increasing with urgency the longer they touched. His hands threaded through her hair, and she stood on the tips of her toes, wanting to get closer to this angel who'd come into her life so unexpectedly and turned everything upside down.

"Gabrielle." His husky voice broke with emotion. "I want to do this all night, but we have to keep moving. I have to keep you safe."

"I know." She kissed him one more time with far more restraint than she thought possible, then pulled back.

"Eat your bread." He wrapped an arm around her. "We can walk for a bit."

"Do you think they're following us?" she asked as they began their slow walk back to Forte Cadence.

"Not anymore." He looked behind and squinted into the darkness. "They can't risk losing anyone else."

"And I can't risk losing you again," she said, wondering if it was the darkness making her so brazen. She'd never so much as held hands with a guy, let alone thrown herself at them like this.

"About that," he said. "The losing me bit…"

"Cassius." She bit down on her lip, wanting to say this right. "I saw a vision of you. Of us."

"I saw it, too." He pulled her tighter. "And it's why I hesitated to return to you. I don't want to cause you pain."

"But what if we can change it?" she asked, certain this was possible. Amba had altered her fate. Gabrielle could do it too.

"We can't." Cassius's voice was so faint she had to strain to hear it. "No matter what we do, it's going to happen."

She shook her head. "It's not. We won't let it. I'll prove it to you."

"Maybe forever isn't meant to be forever," he said. "Maybe forever is more about appreciating what's happening right now."

"I like that." Gabrielle concentrated on this very moment. She had bread in her stomach. The arm of an incredible guy wrapped around her. And she was safe.

Cassius might not be able to promise her a family, and children, gray hair and a future. But he could give her this moment.

"It's our Evernow," she whispered, knowing that whatever hardships she faced in her life, she'd always be able to return to this moment. "Let's live forever, right in the now."

TEN YEARS LATER

CASSIUS

THE NOW

Cassius woke and immediately put his hand to his heart to make sure it was beating. Feeling its strong rhythm, he let out a soft sigh and smiled.

He was still alive.

Better than that, he was still alive with Gabrielle by his side.

He pulled her closer and pressed a kiss to the warmth of her cheek. He'd loved this woman his whole life, even before he'd met her. He was so grateful he'd been able to live long enough to make some precious memories with her.

"Good morning, angel," Gabrielle murmured.

"It's always a good morning with you," he said.

Gabrielle put a hand on his chest and ran her fingers playfully down his sternum. "Long ago, I read my future and saw myself with a husband in a small house with a little garden all of our own."

"Was the husband handsome?" Cassius asked, doing his best to sound serious.

"He was." She grinned. "But not all parts of a vision can be completely accurate…"

Cassius put on a dramatic pout which made Gabrielle laugh. It was his favorite sound in all the kingdoms.

"Then give your ugly husband a kiss." Cassius leaned up on his elbows and pressed his lips to Gabrielle's, never tiring of the way it sent tingles running down his spine. If he searched all the kingdoms, he'd never find anyone like her. She was his one, and his always.

She returned his kiss but swatted him away when he ran his palm down the curve of her waist.

"We have to get to the market." She swung her feet out of their bed. "I'll make some tea."

He let out a sigh as he always did whenever she left his side. He'd spend his entire life connected to her if he could.

Gabrielle crossed to the other side of their little hut and busied herself at the table with what she called tea. Really, it was little more than cold water with a sprig of whatever herb she could scavenge at the market.

Cassius tucked his hands behind his head and watched her. She was still as beautiful as she'd always been. Perhaps even more so now that she was a woman and not a girl. The universe had denied them children, but Cassius wasn't displeased with this. If he wasn't going to be there for his children as they grew up, he wasn't sure it was fair on either a child or Gabrielle for them to go down that path.

He had Gabrielle, and she had him, and that was all they needed.

Since returning to the Valley of the Blessed, life had been even harder than Cassius remembered. Perhaps it was the contrast to his time in The Bay of Laurel where it was possible to forget what the feeling of hunger was. They wanted to go back there, but the Guardians had stopped taking people. The carriage Gabrielle had left on had been the very last one to leave Forte Cadence. They'd even destroyed the bridge that connected the two kingdoms. It seemed the King of The Bay of Laurel was satisfied with the message he'd sent to King Virtus. It was clear who the more powerful ruler was and there was no need for more muscles to be flexed for now.

Gabrielle poured her tea into two cups and brought one over to Cassius as she perched on the side of the bed and looked around proudly at their home.

When Cassius had told his parents he wasn't returning to Aria

Flats, they'd been disappointed. His father hadn't wanted anything more to do with him. But his mother had slipped him a small sum of money, which he'd used to buy this hut. Gabrielle hadn't understood why they couldn't have gone to Aria Flats but he'd been insistent that they remain here. He had the same pull to this place as he'd had to Sage's garden, and he'd learned never to ignore this feeling. There was a reason he and Gabrielle lived in the Valley of the Blessed, even if it wasn't completely apparent now, he believed one day it would be. And despite their hardships, Gabrielle had trusted him on this.

"I love our little house," she said. "But do you know the best part about it?"

He smiled, already knowing what her answer would be but wanting to hear it anyway. "What?"

"You," she said. "I love this house because it's ours. Yours and mine. Which means it has you inside it. I'm so lucky to have found you."

"Pretty sure I found you," he pointed out with a wink.

"Well, then I'm lucky you did." She leaned forward and kissed him softly.

The sound of rain peppered the roof and Gabrielle turned to look forlornly out their small window.

"It's only rain," he told her.

"Do you think we'll get any customers?"

"People always want to know their future," said Cassius. "Rain doesn't wash away curiosity."

She nodded, then took a sip of her tea. They were dependent on their trade from Gabrielle's tent at the market. No longer charging three coins, they bartered with the people, asking them to trade whatever it was that they could spare in exchange for their reading. Sometimes it was bread. Other times it was a coat. Once they were even given a piglet. Gabrielle had quickly re-traded the animal for a bag of walnuts, which she claimed she wasn't going to get attached to and then have to watch die.

Cassius did some of the readings as well now, which pleased Gabrielle, especially when someone entered the tent who made her feel unsafe. He felt good to be able to protect her, but he also worried what would become of her when he was no longer there.

"Stop it," said Gabrielle, frowning at him.

"Stop what?" He drank his tea, avoiding her eye.

"Stop thinking about the future," she said. "We live in the Evernow, remember?"

He nodded. Of course, he remembered. It's just that he also could never forget about the future he knew was looming. She knew it too. No matter how much she insisted she was only living in the moment, he caught the sadness in her eyes when she thought he wasn't looking.

"You're a terrible liar." She set down her empty cup and went to stand up.

He swooped on her, slipping his hand around her waist and pulling her back on the bed, sending the remainder of his tea spilling. "Then punish me."

She shrieked with mock horror and he kissed her, silencing the laughter bubbling at her lips. Her mouth was warm, but the feeling he got when he felt her pressed against him was pure fire.

The market could wait.

If they were going to live in the moment, this was one he intended to fully enjoy.

Gabrielle unbuttoned his shirt and he shrugged it off and closed his eyes as he lay back on the bed.

Right now, the future was an eternity away.

Right now, his future was here.

AURELIA

THE NOW

urelia was tall for her age. But she was smart enough to know this didn't actually make her tall. She was still shorter than her older sister, Lily. And short enough to attract the attention of the people walking through the market.

"Are you okay, dear?" an old lady with black teeth asked. "Where's your mother?"

Ignoring her, Aurelia pulled back her shoulders and stalked ahead, looking for the mysterious tent she'd seen earlier.

Lily was going to murder her when she realized she'd slipped away. They'd promised their parents they were going to stick together. But Lily would never have agreed to let Aurelia go into the tent to see the lady with the pretty hair. When she'd seen her calling out to people who passed, promising to read their future, Aurelia had felt her stomach dip with excitement. It was an opportunity she knew she couldn't miss.

Because if there was one thing Aurelia wanted even more than to be all grown up, it was to know what it was she was supposed to do in this world. Lily's path was set. She'd marry the son of one of their parents' many wealthy friends and have children of her own. She'd have the pick of the bunch. Their mother once said maybe Lily would even end up marrying the Prince. And Aurelia knew what that meant —she'd be left with the scraps like when Lily got to choose what fabric she wanted for a new dress, or which sweet bun to take first from the tray.

Lily always got first choice, and Aurelia had no interest in marrying someone who was little more than a scrap. For once in her life, she wanted to be the important one in the family. The one who got to be the first. Or the smartest. Or the best.

Which was why she needed that fortune telling lady to let her know what she had to do to make that happen.

She spotted the tent up ahead and quickened her pace, wondering how long futures took to be read. It once took Aurelia almost a full week to read a book. Hopefully this was much faster than that. Lily really would kill her if she didn't find her way back to her soon.

The lady was still standing outside her tent. Aurelia walked up to her, tugging on her skirt to get her attention. She looked down and smiled warmly.

"Are you lost, sweetheart?" she asked.

"No." Aurelia shook her head, although in truth she did feel a little lost. Which was the exact reason she was standing here. "I want to know my future."

The lady laughed. Not in a mean way, but still, it made Aurelia feel a little upset. Why didn't anybody take children seriously? They had ideas and thoughts and feelings just like grown ups. They knew stuff! Aurelia knew lots of stuff.

She slipped around the lady and into her tent.

The woman followed her, raising her brows when Aurelia sat at her table and stared at the crystal ball. Her fingers itched to lift the cloth that was covering it to take a peek. She'd never in her life seen a real crystal ball before.

"What are you doing here?" the lady asked.

"You said you read futures." Aurelia wondered if perhaps this woman was a little thick. Wasn't it obvious what she was doing here? "And I'm a customer."

The lady smiled, as if amused. "I don't read the futures of children."

Aurelia reached into her pocket and produced the silver coin her mother had given her for emergencies. She was going to have to pretend she lost it when she got home. Although, really, this *was* an emergency. There were things she needed to know.

The lady's eyes widened at the sight of the coin. "Where did you get this?"

Aurelia shrugged, not wanting to tell her anything more than she had to. If this woman was any good at her job she should know where she got this coin.

The lady studied her, and Aurelia became self-conscious of her finely made clothes and shoes. She was aware her family had more than most in Forte Cadence. That's what happened when your father did business with the King. Not that Aurelia had any idea what business that was, but she hoped one day to find out. Maybe this lady would tell her that right now.

The lady sat on the other side of the table and took the coin, slipping it into the pocket of her tattered dress. "My name's Gabrielle."

Aurelia smiled, happy to have a name to put to her face. "I'm Aurelia."

"Tell me, Aurelia." Gabrielle stretched out her hands, one on each side of her crystal ball. "Why does someone so young wish to know what future lies ahead?"

"Isn't that the whole point?" Aurelia tilted her head, genuinely confused. "What's the use in finding out your future when you're too old to do anything about it?"

Gabrielle laughed. "I suppose so. But are you sure you want to know? Sometimes it's better not to."

A sadness crossed Gabrielle's blue eyes and Aurelia wondered what she'd found out that she hadn't wanted to know. But this was supposed to be about Aurelia, so she didn't ask.

"Put your hands in mine," Gabrielle said.

Aurelia felt a thrill race through her, like the doors to a secret world were about to open to her. She put her hands in Gabrielle's and watched her close her eyes tightly as if concentrating on something very difficult.

Seconds passed and Aurelia tried to keep her feet from jiggling, which is something her mother told her she did when she was being impatient.

Gabrielle's eyes moved behind her eyelids like she was dreaming and Aurelia really hoped she hadn't fallen asleep. But people didn't normally sleep sitting up in chairs. Then Gabrielle let out a gasp and her eyes popped open and she let go of Aurelia's hands.

"What is it?" Aurelia asked.

Gabrielle wiped her palms on her skirt and gave her one of those smiles grown-ups do when they don't want you to know something.

"I paid for my future," said Aurelia, trying to sound like her father when he was being bossy. "Tell it to me. Please?"

"I can't." Gabrielle looked to the dirt floor of her tent as she chewed on her lip.

"Why can't you?" Aurelia leaned forward.

Gabrielle didn't seem to want to answer this, convincing Aurelia even more that she'd seen something terrible.

"I'm not going to get married, am I?" said Aurelia, trying not to sound like she was whining. "Or maybe I am and I'm going to get one of Lily's scraps."

Gabrielle lifted her gaze and looked across the table at Aurelia. Her eyes were spilling over with tears that she was blinking away.

Aurelia gasped, realizing her future must be worse than marrying a scrap.

"I'm going to die young," she whispered. "You saw me die, didn't you?"

Gabrielle shook her head firmly. "You're not going to die young. I saw you married with four beautiful children who you love very much."

Aurelia shuddered as she took this in. Four children. That sounded like quite a lot. Twice more than her own mother had. She wasn't sure she wanted that many children, let alone to have to do the thing that made them. Four times no less! But what Gabrielle had told her didn't sound like upsetting news, which meant she hadn't told her everything.

"My husband is a scrap, isn't he?" she asked. "He's one of Lily's leftovers."

Gabrielle shook her head as she reached for Aurelia's hands. "Are you sure you want to know?"

"Yes," Aurelia whispered, holding her breath as she waited.

Gabrielle grimaced. "Your husband will be King Virtus."

Aurelia pulled back her hands in shock, accidentally pulling the cloth off the crystal ball, revealing it was nothing more than a rock.

"You're a fake," she said. "This isn't a real crystal ball. And King Virtus is about a million years old. I can't be marrying him. You're making this up."

"The rock is fake, I admit." Gabrielle pulled the cloth back over it. "But I can assure you I'm not. Honestly, right now I wish that I were."

"But I can't marry an old man." Aurelia tried to stand but her legs felt a bit shaky, so she remained on her seat.

"It won't be the King Virtus that you know," said Gabrielle. "The King Virtus you'll marry is his son. The Prince. He'll become King one day, and you'll stand beside him as his Queen."

These words changed everything. They had Aurelia's back straightening and her heart pounding, no longer with fear or uncertainty, but excitement.

"I'm going to be the Queen of Forte Cadence?" she asked, needing to check she'd heard correctly. "And Prince Virtus will be my husband?"

"That's what I saw," said Gabrielle softly.

"But I don't understand." Aurelia kneaded her hands in her lap. "That's wonderful news. The Prince isn't a scrap. He's the best prize there is."

She'd seen the Prince once when her father had taken her to the Palace and while he wasn't the most handsome boy, he was…well, he was the Prince. One day he'd be the most powerful man in all the Kingdom. And given Forte Cadence was the largest kingdom of them all, that meant he'd be the most powerful man in all the world. And she'd be his Queen. Nobody would ever be able to tell her what to do ever again. Except for the King, of course. But he was her husband, which meant he'd love her, so she didn't need to worry about that.

"He's definitely a prize," said Gabrielle, although her voice still sounded more sad than excited. Was she envious?

"And you're sure it was me?" Aurelia asked. "Not my sister? Lily looks exactly like me, only older."

"It was you," she said. "I'm so sorry."

Aurelia stood. She needed to get back to Lily before their mother found out she went missing. She had to stay out of trouble and be good. Always. Otherwise, the Prince might find out and not want to marry her.

"Thank you for the reading," she said, remembering her manners.

Gabrielle nodded, wiping away another tear that had slipped down her cheek.

Aurelia skipped out of the tent feeling far taller than when she'd entered it. She was going to be Queen of Forte Cadence.

Which meant she'd be the first.

The smartest.

And the best.

GABRIELLE

THE NOW

Gabrielle was unable to stand from her table after what she'd just seen.

That poor child.

Of all the people to come into her tent, it had to be the future Queen. And Aurelia had such a beautiful soul, which made it even worse. That evil Prince was going to eat her alive when he got his hands on her. Possibly literally.

She shuddered, remembering the day she'd hidden in the hen house and seen him kill the chicken, then take great pleasure in plucking out its feathers. The hen was only lucky he'd done things in that order. That boy's soul was the opposite of Aurelia's. Even worse than his own father's, and that was saying something.

Cassius came into the tent with a concerned expression.

"Was that girl okay?" he asked, sounding a little out of breath. "She's a little young to be wandering the markets alone."

Gabrielle nodded. "She's okay. For now."

Cassius sat on the stool the future Queen had only just vacated and waited for her to explain. They didn't usually share the details of readings they did, especially if they knew the person, but sometimes it was necessary.

Like today.

"She came for a reading," said Gabrielle, feeling for the silver coin in her pocket.

"But we don't read for children." Cassius's brow furrowed, an expression that only deepened as she slid the coin across the table to him. "You didn't take this from her, did you?"

Gabrielle shrugged, her cheeks pinking up. "I thought if I took it, I could buy a dozen eggs and share them with those in need. She'd have plenty of eggs already in the home she comes from."

Cassius slid the coin back to her and nodded his understanding. "And what did you see? A rich husband? A stable full of horses?"

"King Virtus," she said on a whimper. "She's going to grow up and marry the Prince. She'll become our Queen."

Cassius's head spun back to the entrance of the tent as if he expected to catch another glimpse of the small girl.

"We have to stop her," he said, getting to his feet. "Hurry. We can catch her if we're fast."

"Cassius, no!" Gabrielle held up a hand. "We can't change the future."

"But we have to try." He ran a hand through his hair. "We can't let her marry that monster."

"Someone will marry him," Gabrielle said firmly. "Wouldn't you rather it was someone with a good heart? Someone who can bring some good to our kingdom, instead of letting it be ruled solely by evil?"

These words had Cassius's steps pausing as he let out a groan.

"She'll have a daughter," said Gabrielle, revealing something she hadn't told Aurelia. She learned long ago that not everything she saw needed to be told. "Her daughter will have a heart spun from gold and the power to change the world. We can't stop her from being born."

"So, we just let her go?" Cassius paced the tent. "We let her grow up and marry a monster, all for the greater good?"

Gabrielle nodded slowly. "I hate it as much as you do. But...the alternative would be far worse. Many more will die if Aurelia doesn't become our Queen. Her daughter needs to be born."

There was a movement at the entrance to the tent and Aurelia stepped back inside. Gabrielle gasped, hoping she hadn't heard too much.

Aurelia cast her eyes down and fiddled with the sash on her dress.

"Aurelia," Gabrielle said gently. "Are you okay? Are you lost?"

"I'm sorry to interrupt." Aurelia glanced shyly up at Cassius. "I didn't know you had another customer."

"I'll wait outside," said Cassius, not correcting her about his relationship to Gabrielle. He slipped out of the tent, giving Aurelia a sympathetic smile on his way out.

"What is it?" Gabrielle went to Aurelia and put a hand on her arm, aware that to do this in the future would be considered a break in royal protocol.

"I was happy when I left here," said Aurelia. "But then I remembered something that I had to ask you about. You were sad. If you really did see my future as Queen, why would that make you sad?"

Gabrielle summoned all the energy she possessed to pull up a smile to her lips. "I was just surprised. It's not every day I have the future Queen walk into my tent."

"So, there's nothing bad about me marrying the Prince?" Aurelia asked, proving she was smart as well as doomed to a life of misery.

"You're going to have four beautiful children," Gabrielle reminded her as she knelt down to Aurelia's height. "And stylish dresses, and expensive jewels around your neck, and the best food in all the kingdom."

All of this was true. And it was always far better to stick to the truth.

Aurelia smiled to hear this. "So, you're sure you were just surprised?"

Gabrielle nodded. She had most definitely been surprised. "Please, promise me you'll come back and see me again when you're Queen. There are things I can tell you that might help."

"Help with what?" Aurelia bit down on her lip.

"Just help," said Gabrielle. "You can call on me if ever you need me."

"But if I'm the Queen, why would I need anybody else?" Aurelia asked. "Apart from my husband."

Gabrielle tried to hold the smile on her face, begging her tears not to fall. "We all need somebody sometimes. Even those of us with rich and powerful husbands."

"Thank you." Aurelia straightened her back, looking every bit the future Queen she was. "You can be my secret. If you tell me what to do, then I can be the best Queen ever."

"I'd love that." Gabrielle stood and guided Aurelia to the door. "And I hope to see you again one day, Your Royal Highness."

Aurelia giggled, seeming to like the sound of that. She left the tent and Gabrielle watched her scamper down the road, her eyes darting left and right as she searched for whoever she'd come here with.

"How did I do?" Gabrielle asked Cassius as he stepped around the side of the tent.

"You think I was listening in?" He pulled his face into an expression of mock horror.

"I know you were." She let out a sigh and smiled.

He put his arm around her and led her back inside. "Of course I listened in. And of course you were wonderful. I'm proud of you, my Angel."

The tears she'd been holding at bay threatened to spill once more. "But I'm not proud of myself."

"No." Cassius pulled her to his chest. "Don't say that. You've brought so much good to this world. And there's so much more to come. You've seen it. I have, too. What you do is so important."

She balled her hands into fists at his chest. "But what's the use? If we can't change the future, why should we even try? Maybe it's time to pack away this tent."

"We may not be able to change the future," he said, looking concerned. "But I believe we can bend it a little. Just look at me. I'm still here, aren't I?"

She nodded, thinking of the visions they'd had over the years of his death. She knew it had to be coming soon but tried not to dwell on it.

She couldn't bear to ruin any of the remaining time they had left, mourning him before he was even gone.

"There's something else I discovered this morning while you were with our future Queen," he said. "It was the reason I came running back here in the first place."

"What is it?" She looked up at him, hoping it was something good. She'd seen enough evil for one day.

He slipped his hand into hers and led her outside. "Come on. It's better if you see it for yourself."

CASSIUS

THE NOW

*C*assius held Gabrielle's hand as he led her through the market streets. The timing was perfect. He refused to call it a coincidence, having long ago given up believing that such a thing existed. What he'd seen—or rather who he'd seen—had been meant to happen that very morning. Because there was no way Gabrielle could lose faith in her gift. And once she saw what he had to show her, she'd feel better than ever about the potential of what she could offer the world.

"I'm not keen on surprises," she muttered beside him. "I wish you'd just tell me what's going on."

He grinned at her, not giving anything away.

They reached the end of the market and followed the street to a row of houses on the other side to where their own home stood. While ramshackle and cobbled together from scraps, these homes were luxurious compared to those of the people who lived in their market tents like Gabrielle used to.

"Do you remember years ago you told me about a woman with a goat?" Cassius asked her.

"Oh." She turned pale. "Please don't take me to her. Her son is probably dead by now and she'll say it was all my fault."

"Do you also remember that the boy's father was with me when I was taken to The Bay of Laurel?" he asked as they approached a small house.

She nodded. "You said his name was Gregor. But you were never able to find his family when you returned here."

"That's right." Excitement built within him. "Well, I saw Gregor at the market this morning."

Gabrielle slowed her steps as they walked up the short path to the front door. "But how is that possible? Nobody ever came back from The Bay of Laurel. Apart from you."

"Gregor said once his training was complete, the Guardians offered to release him if he didn't wish to remain with them," Cassius explained, raising his hand and knocking on the flimsy door. "It turns out nobody was ever a captive in the first place. Gregor was one of the very rare ones who chose to return."

"He really did love his son," Gabrielle said, understanding at once. Life was so difficult in Forte Cadence, it was hard to believe why anyone would choose to return. But sometimes it was more important to fill your belly with love than food. Cassius knew Gabrielle understood that.

Gregor opened the front door of the house. Cassius smiled at his old friend. It was wonderful to see him in such good shape. He had a firm layer of muscle on his body and pink in his cheeks, making him seem years younger than when Cassius had known him, despite a decade having passed. Gabrielle stared at him, clearly not used to seeing anyone in such good health.

"Gabrielle, this is Gregor," said Cassius, hardly able to believe the moment had come where he could introduce them. "Gregor, this is Gabrielle. I was just explaining to her that you'd chosen to return home."

"That's right." Gregor gave Gabrielle a warm smile. "I wanted to see my son. He was so unwell when I left."

"Did he..." Gabrielle's words trailed off and she tried again. "Is your son..."

"I'm alive," said a young man, stepping out from behind Gregor. "My name's Blaize."

Cassius drank in the sight of this young man, having heard so much about him but never having met him in person. While he didn't look nearly as healthy as his father, for a resident of Forte Cadence he was doing well. Tall and lean, his skin was clear and it looked like he still had most of his teeth.

Gregor reached out and took Gabrielle's hand. "We're very grateful for how you tried to warn us."

Gabrielle returned his smile, politely taking back her hand. Cassius knew this was to avoid the visions that would have poured into her mind. Sometimes it was hard to really put yourself in the now when your mind seemed determined to live in the tomorrow.

"I'm so pleased," said Gabrielle. "Although, I'm not sure my warnings did very much. Your wife didn't seem ready to listen."

"Come in and we'll explain." Gregor ushered them into his home, which was one large room with some mattresses on one side, leaning up against the wall, and some implements for cooking on the other.

A woman who Cassius assumed must be Gregor's wife was standing at a table wiping her hands repetitively on her apron.

"It's wonderful to meet you at last," said Cassius, remembering his manners.

The woman nodded but her gaze remained fixed on Gabrielle.

"I'm afraid I owe you an apology," she said.

"Me?" Gabrielle pressed her palm to her chest.

"You told me not to give our son our goat's milk and I refused to believe you." Gregor's wife let go of her apron to wring her hands. "Then Gregor was taken by the Guardians and life got even more difficult. I couldn't feed the goat and her milk dried up. The butcher took her for a small sum. And…" She buried her face in her hands.

"And then I got better," Blaize said, finishing the story for her. "I was able to keep my food down, which meant I got stronger."

"It was all my fault," Gregor's wife sobbed. "I should have listened to you. Instead, I took back the bread from you and told everyone you were a fraud."

"It's okay," Gabrielle said, seeming to mean it. Her forgiving heart was one of the reasons Cassius loved her so much. "Sometimes the truth is difficult to hear. You just weren't ready."

Gregor's wife raced forward and pulled Gabrielle into a hug.

"I'm so sorry," she sobbed. "I should have apologized to you long ago, but I was too ashamed. So, I've been sending people to your tent instead, trying to make it up to you."

Gabrielle gave Cassius an amused look. At least now they knew why their business had been thriving.

"You have nothing to be sorry for," said Gabrielle, returning her hug. "I've been fine. And I'm happy your family is all so well. And now reunited."

Gregor's wife released Gabrielle, looking like a great weight had been lifted.

Cassius put a hand on Gabrielle's back, wanting her to understand why he brought her here. "Do you see it now?" he asked her. "You can help people. What you do is important. You can't give up. Not now. Not ever."

She nodded at him, seeming to believe him. The gift Gabrielle had been bestowed with wasn't always a blessing, but it was most definitely a gift.

Gregor cleared his throat and Cassius turned to him, surprised to see such a serious expression on his face.

"Cassius, I'm afraid there's something else I have to tell you. And you might want to sit down for this."

GABRIELLE

THE NOW

*G*abrielle instinctively drew closer to Cassius at Gregor's words. They sat down on two small stools and braced themselves for whatever it was he had to tell them.

It had been wonderful to meet Blaize and see that he'd grown into a strong young man. For him to have his father back in his life must feel like a real bonus. It was an interesting strategy by the King of the Bay of Laurel—to recruit an army by force, then treat them so well that they became loyal by choice. Aside from Gregor, of course. And there must surely be others like him. Although, Gabrielle doubted any of them would fight too hard against an army of Guardians if they were to invade.

"What is it?" Cassius asked, leaning forward.

Gregor sat across the table from them and hung his head as a sadness crossed his eyes.

"Not long after you left, your bed in the hut we lived in was taken by a young man called Lark," he said.

"Lark!" Gabrielle smiled. "He was on the carriage with me. He was quite taken with my friend Amba. Did you see her, too?"

Gregor nodded, but not in a way that brought Gabrielle any joy.

She crossed her arms and sat back, bracing herself for what she was about to hear.

"Lark was in love with Amba." Gregor gave a half-smile. "They asked the Guardians for permission to promise themselves to each other and share a hut. This was granted and they were very happy together. Amba often spoke of you, Gabrielle, and how grateful she was to you for changing the direction of her life."

"She needed to leave the palace," she whispered, fearing this story was about to take a turn. "Her husband was a violent man."

"And determined," said Gregor. "I woke one night to a loud scream. It was Amba. There was a man standing over her calling her his wife. I tried to stop him, but…"

Cassius took Gabrielle's hand and squeezed it. "Go on," he whispered.

"He had a dagger." Gregor swallowed. "I'm afraid he'd already used it to kill them both."

A harrowed sob forced its way up and out of Gabrielle's mouth as her hands flew to her lips. She'd seen this very scene when she'd read Jaff's future outside the palace grounds. And she'd tried to change it, not only by telling Jaff that to carry out this murderous act would bring him bad fortune, but she'd removed Amba from his reach. It seemed evil doesn't recognize borders. He'd tracked her down anyway, probably even more determined having been told by Gabrielle what he shouldn't do. The man was as stubborn as he was vindictive.

"Do you still think I can help people?" Gabrielle sobbed, turning her gaze to Cassius, who looked equally distressed. "All I did was make things worse."

"That's not true," said Gregor. "They were happy. Lark and Amba had some wonderful years together. Had you not rescued Amba from her husband, I'm sure she'd have died far sooner, and her final years would have been lived in fear and misery."

Gabrielle nodded, even though she wasn't sure she agreed. "And Lark? He'd never have met Amba if it weren't for me."

"You convinced him to surrender to the Guardians and allow

himself to be taken in their carriage," said Gregor. "He'd have likely fallen ill and died here had he not had the opportunity to be fed and healed in The Bay of Laurel."

"Not everyone here dies," she whispered.

"He would have gone anyway," said Cassius. "The Guardians would have captured him and taken him by force. You saw it in your vision. He was meant to be there. All you did was remove the fear when it happened. And it was a path that led him to great love. That's worth something."

This made Gabrielle feel a little better. That she could believe. Lark was meant to go to The Bay of Laurel. It was his destiny. Exactly like it was Jaff's to end his life. It seemed destiny wasn't always about what was right and just.

"What happened to him?" Cassius asked. "The man who killed them."

Gregor glanced at his wife and son, seeming reluctant to talk. "Let's just say he won't be hurting anyone ever again."

"Bad fortune," Gabrielle murmured, realizing what she'd told Jaff had come true.

Cassius, who knew the story, heard her and nodded his agreement. "You warned him. He didn't listen. And it most definitely brought him bad luck."

"Not luck," growled Gregor. "He got what was coming to him."

"Gregor!" his wife gasped.

Gregor shifted uncomfortably in his chair.

"We might leave you," said Gabrielle, needing some time of her own to process what they'd been told. Clearly this family had a lot to talk about as well. "We'll be sure to come back again soon."

"Please do." Gregor smiled at them. "Our home is your home. If there's anything you need, you just let us know."

"That's very generous of you." Gabrielle glanced around at their meagre belongings. "Thank you."

Gabrielle straightened her dress as she stood. Cassius went to Gregor and gave his old friend a hug. As he did so, Gabrielle took the silver coin that Aurelia had given her from her pocket and placed it in a wide crack in the table, so that the top was just poking up.

These people needed it more than she did, and they'd never accept it if she tried to give it to them. Let them find it one day and wonder where it came from. She owed them that much after all the business Gregor's wife had passed her way.

They walked back to the tent in silence, the air feeling far heavier than it had on the way there. Back then she'd been weighed down by curiosity.

Now she was weighed down by grief.

CASSIUS

THE NOW

*C*assius couldn't sleep no matter how hard he tried. The night grew old as the moon crossed the sky and still he was awake. His death was drawing near. He'd already cheated time and was somehow still alive to lie beside the most beautiful woman to walk the earth. One day, they would dance across the sky together. But for now, he was grateful to be able to hold his hand made from flesh against the warmth of her body.

His visions had been getting more frequent as his time was drawing near. Only now he dreamed of the kingdoms.

He saw people in robes lining up and whispering their wishes, their voices rising as one into the sky.

He saw a lush garden in bloom, with an alchemist picking flowers and turning them into powerful elixirs that could heal the body and control the mind.

He saw people living in a harsh desert, banned from one of humanity's most important pleasures—the simple act of placing their hands on each other.

He saw the Guardians grow stronger, then weaken, as a mysterious force gripped them, threatening to bring their kingdom down.

And he saw a girl trapped in a bejewelled castle in the middle of an angry sea, being held captive by a force not even she could understand.

He knew all of these visions had one thing in common. They called on the people to harness the power of one of the human senses.

Touch. Sight. Taste. Hearing. Scent.

And while each kingdom would face a battle of their own, it wouldn't be until they united and learned to use all their senses together that happiness could ever be found.

He kept these visions from Gabrielle, knowing she had her own important role to play in all of this. One that needed her to focus on the kingdom that had always been her home.

Aurelia would become Queen. And Gabrielle would be her most powerful advisor. Except the path that lay ahead for Gabrielle would be one of the most difficult anyone had ever walked.

But she was strong. And brave. And she could face whatever life threw at her. Because she would know that it was how it was meant to be.

She'd find peace in her heart as she'd know she sent Aurelia to a life built on fear and sadness because it was for the greater good. And Gabrielle would never ask something of someone that she wasn't prepared to do herself.

Cassius wriggled down under the covers of their bed and wrapped his arm around Gabrielle.

"You're my biggest, greatest love," he whispered.

She didn't hear him. But she didn't need to. Because she already knew it with all her senses.

Most importantly, she knew it with her heart.

GABRIELLE

THE NOW

*G*abrielle stirred. This time of the day was the most difficult. It was that in between time when she was still gripped by the oblivion of sleep, but threads of awareness started to creep in. Threads that reminded her that her days of sleeping beside Cassius were numbered. That one day soon she'd wake and find a cold place in the bed where his warmth had once been.

She put an arm around him, checking for the rise and fall of his chest, holding her own breath while she did so. Feeling his chest move, she let out a soft sigh of relief, wondering if he realized that was why she did this each morning. Probably. But then again, he also seemed surprised to find himself alive each morning when the visions of his death had been so clear.

Cassius pulled her closer and she breathed him in.

It was a difficult life she'd chosen for herself, tying herself to a man she knew would never know what it was like to have wrinkles on his handsome face. But she wouldn't have it any other way. It hadn't even felt like a choice. Once she met Cassius, her soul was tied to him forever.

Just like Lark and Amba, it was better to have known true love and have had some precious years basking in its warmth, than to live her entire life feeling safe from hurt yet with her heart left cold. Whatever happened in the future, she wouldn't do anything any differently.

And whatever happened after Cassius was gone, she would face it with courage. She knew hard times lay before her. But she also believed that one day she'd play an important part in turning the bad into good.

"I love you now. I love you forever," she whispered. "You're my Evernow."

"My Evernow," he murmured back.

As he held her tightly, she knew it was true.

No matter who and no matter what. This moment, right now, belonged to her.

THE END

Ready to discover The Kingdoms of Evernow?

Check out Book 1, The Whisperers of Evernow!

http://mybook.to/hcwhisperers

THE WHISPERERS OF EVERNOW

BOOK 1 THE KINGDOMS OF EVERNOW

Five kingdoms. Five senses. One secret that will change them all.

★★★★★ "A highly enjoyable fantastical joy ride."

Manipulated by a vicious King, Jeremiah is stripped of his identity and forced into a life of silent submission as a Whisperer. Allowed only to speak at the command of the King, one thousand Whisperers must line up in rows and chant their sadistic ruler's darkest desires. As each evil wish comes true, the King's power over his impoverished kingdom grows.

When Jeremiah's fears for the family he left behind are confirmed, he turns in desperation to the most unlikely person for help—the King's eldest daughter. But is Princess Rose as kind as she is beautiful, or will she lure him into a trap?

To save those dearest to him, Jeremiah has no choice but to put his trust in Rose, whose own life is threatened as her father prepares to clear the path to the throne for his newborn son. Together, they embark on a bold plan to overthrow the King and set the Whisperers free.

As love blossoms in this most unlikely place, Jeremiah and Rose must discover how to use the power of the spoken word to conquer more than just the kingdom. They will need to conquer their hearts.

The first full-length book in the spellbinding The Kingdoms of Evernow series, this is a must-read by award-winning author, Heidi Catherine.

Grab your copy now!

http://mybook.to/hcwhisperers

ALSO BY HEIDI CATHERINE

The Kingdoms of Evernow

Five kingdoms. Five senses.

One secret that will change them all.

The Kingdoms of Evernow (Prequel)

The Whisperers of Evernow

The Alchemists of Evernow

The Empress of Evernow

The Guardians of Evernow

The Angels of Evernow

The Soulweaver series

Two girls. Two lives. One soul.

The Soulweaver

The Truthseeker

The Shadowmaker

The Sovereign Code

Humans saved bees from extinction...

and created the deadliest threat we've seen yet

Harvest Day

Hive Mind

Queen Hunt

Venom Rising

Sting Wars

Elemental Games

Elemental powers. Deadly games. No escape.

Elemental Games

Elemental Uprising

Elemental Wars

Elemental Solution

The Thaw Chronicles

Four tests. Seven days. Nine teens.

Only the chosen shall breed.

Burning (Prequel)

Rising

Breaking

Falling

Reckoning

Extant

Exist

Exile

Expose

Tournaments of Thaw

Conquer the Thaw

The Oasis Trials

The Oasis Deception

The Last Oasis

WANT TO STAY IN TOUCH?

Heidi loves to connect with readers, so please say hello on social media, leave a review on Amazon or Goodreads, or visit her at www. heidicatherine.com

facebook.com/HeidiCatherineAuthor
instagram.com/HeidiCatherine
tiktok.com/@heidicatherineauthor
amazon.com/author/heidicatherine

ABOUT THE AUTHOR

Heidi writes fantasy and dystopian novels, which gives her a chance to escape into worlds vastly different to her own life in the burbs. While she quite enjoys killing her characters (especially the awful ones), she promises she's far better behaved in real life. Other than writing and reading, Heidi's current obsessions include watching far too much reality TV with the excuse that it's research for her books.